GW00363370

By the same authors:
Toon Tales – a Euro-Geordie pilgrimage
© 2004 ISBN 0-9548357-0-0
Toon Odyssey – the pilgrimage goes on
© 2005 ISBN 0-9548357-1-9
Toon Publishing Ltd

Lordenshaw

by
Barry Robertson
in co-authorship with
Peter Cain

To Neale
Best wishes

Barry
and Pete

First published in Great Britain in 2007 by
Toon Publishing Limited
129/131 New Bridge Street
Newcastle upon Tyne NE1 2SW

e-mail: toonpublishing@yahoo.co.uk
website: http://www.freewebs.com/toonpublishing/

1 3 5 7 9 10 8 6 4 2

A CIP catalogue record for this book is available from the British Library

ISBN(10) 0-9548357-2-7
ISBN(13) 978 0954835729

Printed and bound in Great Britain
by Biddles Ltd, King's Lynn, Norfolk

Contents

Acknowledgments

Our many thanks go to Malcolm Colling, Chris Birch, and Phil Rhodes for advice, inspiration, technical and musical knowledge, and proof-reading.

FOREWORD

You have in your hands the re-telling of an ancient, but only latterly rediscovered Northumbrian legend. The book is set in real places of the present and the past, both near and far, and often co-existing. It's a wonderful place to be - where the writer has the power to choose between following or changing the course of history! And what power you, too, the reader, have to create your own personal meaning out of the words on these pages.

At the end of this book, the mystery will be revealed to you in its original version. But first, let Dodd Law accompany you in the wake of our heroine Linn Rorting in her timeless quest through the Northumbria of the distant past and present to far-flung ancient sites in search of lost laments, stolen stones and enigmatic markings.

CHAPTER ONE - GONE

"Why didn't you come to report this earlier?"

The coffee at Market Street Police Station is bitter. And weak. Why can't we make real coffee in this country? Especially at times like this, you need a good solid dose of caffeine. Or of something, and this is nothing. Just coloured hot water. I'm drinking it, and I'm up to my neck in it too, if the looks on their faces are anything to go by. But reaching for my cup and taking another sip gives me a few precious moments to think.

Almost three weeks had passed and I had plumbed the depths of despair. The monotony was stultifying. Gave me a lot of unwanted time to dwell on things and torture myself. Still, at least the routine was there to give some sort of framework for my day. Get up at six, leave the flat in Hanover Street at seven and make my way across the city centre on the Quayside Q2 bus and then the 22 to be at my desk on Scotswood Road by about a quarter to eight.

"I suppose it was because I still don't think that she's what you would term 'missing', as in something has befallen her, or that she is in hiding. You see, I thought she'd be back any day... any minute really. I still do. But finally I thought I had to try to do something actively to find her, rather than just wait for her to return."

And because I couldn't accept that she had gone. Left me. Left everything. Just took up and left. But gone where? Bulgaria? Bratislava? Bergen? I had no idea. I'd even been so desperate that I'd gone looking for the mad piper. I was sure he knew something, somehow. But he was nowhere to be seen either. It was as if he'd vanished into thin air. Or gone underground.

Every day, lunch was around twelve-thirty. No more pie and a pint in the Crooked Billet. And the canteen was never appealing. Just a walk along by the river. Not the prettiest section of the Tyne, this. But calming and soothing as always. The factories almost down to the water's edge. Up the banks on either side, endless red-brick terraced streets where my great-grandparents had lived and my granda had been born. To the east the reassuring sight of Newcastle and Gateshead's bridges, and to the west the first hints of the Tyne Valley's beauty. As if nothing had happened, as if nothing had ever happened. Not ever. Just sliding by. As always. Just as it had done before even the Romans arrived. Just as it did while they were here those three and a half centuries or so. And just as it did after they had left, and the Angles and Saxons and Vikings had arrived.

The door opened and the second detective, the inspector, came back in with a portly man in a well-cut black suit. The stranger approached me with an appraising look and a thin smile and shook my hand almost reluctantly, it seemed to me.

"Ah! Mister... sorry, do excuse me... Doctor Law, good morning. My name is Doctor Ingram. I happened to be in the building this morning to discuss another case. I'm a clinical psychologist by profession and the constabulary calls upon me from time to time to give expert advice. They asked if I'd mind sitting in with you for a short while. I trust this will be acceptable to you?"

Why am I 'another case' all of a sudden? I only came in to report a missing person. And why do they think they need a psychologist to talk to me? Do they think I'm crazy or something? I find myself nodding my agreement to this rather pompous-looking man while I am still turning these thoughts over in my head. Acquiescing too easily again. It's what happens when I'm faced with figures of authority, and especially when I find myself in a predicament that I've never experienced before.

"No, I have no objection at all, Doctor," I stutter out, adding unconvincingly, "Anything you can do to help find Linn would be much appreciated." I hope that gives him a good hint that I don't think I'm in need of help from a psychologist or psychiatrist or whatever he said he was.

In the evenings I had sometimes taken off in the car. Out to Rothbury, to Lordenshaw. Kidding myself I might find her there. And right enough, I often found her there, but only in my dreams. And they were getting more and more like hers. But all there was in my waking time was the outline of the walls, the rocks, their shadows, and the heather in full bloom and bathed in the Northumbrian sunset. Kissed by the gentlest of westerly breezes growing more eager as it approached its first taste of the North Sea. I would always come across some sightseers and a few walkers - the old lady with her dog among their number. We would stop and chat and it turned out she was a bit of a birdwatcher. She would point them out to me – dippers and sandpipers, wheaters and wagtails, kestrels and sparrowhawks, merlin and peregrines, and the occasional curlew. It's the symbol of the Northumberland National Park. But she could never point out the bird who'd flown north-east and away.

I had usually driven back via Hexham, coming back into Newcastle on the A69, driving right through the centre, or sometimes past Gallowgate, just to make sure everything was in its place. Which of course it wasn't. Not with Linn gone.

"Thank you, Doctor Law. In which case, for all of our benefits, could I ask you to go over again what you have been telling my colleagues this morning? It's all a little puzzling and I think it would benefit from another telling."

LORDENSHAW

Against my better judgment I reach for my cup again and take a gulp from its murky depths. The congealed coffee whitener peels loose from the bottom of the cup and I gag as it slides across the rim and impacts stickily on the back of my throat.

At least it gives me some more thinking space but I waste it fixating on the tone of his voice when he addressed me as 'Doctor'. As if he doesn't believe a chemist can be a 'proper' doctor like he obviously believes himself to be. As the police might say, I am rapidly forming a dislike for 'our Mister Ingram'. Another fault of mine, forming opinions too quickly, based on first impressions.

"You say she works part-time in schools. Doing what, exactly?"

They must have missed her, surely. But it was on a supply basis. Perhaps she had finished a contract for a couple of mornings, and that was it. They contact an agency saying they need a teacher for this or that subject on this day or that, and the agency tries to get in touch with a suitable teacher. And if they couldn't get hold of one, they simply tried for another. This is the competitive marketplace. Those had been her exact words. Nobody gives a damn about anybody else. As long as the figures balance, everybody's happy. Apart from the kids, that is. They are always the ones who lose out.

"She does supply work. You know, a morning here and an afternoon there. Kind of freelance, I suppose you'd call it. History, local history mainly. Acts as an educator on field-trips, she says. I've

7

seen her in action – she really gets into her role, makes you believe she was actually there when these ancient sites were in full swing. Class trips to the Roman Wall, the Segedunum Roman fort in Wallsend, Durham Cathedral. You know, that sort of thing."

"Bronze age hill-forts as well?"

This time it was one of the policemen asking the question. And his tone was different, harsher. More knowing. It was the detective inspector, more smartly dressed than the detective sergeant. Wearing a suit and tie, not jeans and sweatshirt. But I suppose a detective's dress code changes with his particular assignment. Maybe the inspector had just been to court while the sergeant, Detective Sergeant Humbleton, had been out scouring Newcastle's less salubrious watering holes looking for some villain or other. I was sure I could smell drink on him.

Well-spoken, the inspector was. Barely a trace of Geordie, but a trace there was. There always is. Detective Inspector Breamish, or maybe Beamish, I think they had said his name was. He had asked his question with his back to me as he stood at the window looking down at Newcastle's mid-morning traffic. Second floor I think we were on. We had all been distracted by the tooting of horns and he had gone over to see what was going on. It was clear from his manner that he always had to know exactly what was happening.

"Yes, those hill-forts as well. In fact she's quite an expert. And they're Iron Age actually, not that it will affect your enquiries, I don't think."

I could feel my voice was trembling a bit now, so I coughed and took a sip of water. Nice of them to give me a choice of coffee and water, though by now they were equally tepid. She had recently looked after a school trip to Lordenshaw hill-fort. For Willington Quay and Wylam Primary Schools. She had been so very impressed by the discipline and the interest the kids had taken. Even though one or two of them had had to be told to take the earphones out of their ears and switch off their mobiles. It had been a really windy day and she'd had to shout at the top of her voice at one stage. And low-flying RAF jets on exercise over the Otterburn training range hadn't helped either. It was so important to know the history of your home region, she'd said. You had to know your roots, otherwise you couldn't possibly understand who, or the way, you were yourself.

What about those whose people had come from elsewhere, I had objected, the Irish for example? Tens of thousands of them had poured into Tyneside in the late nineteenth century to work in the pits, the shipyards and the chemical and steel works. Jarrow had been a tiny village mid-century but by 1900 it was a Klondike boomtown thanks to Palmers shipyard and the steelworks. People still call it Little Ireland. And all the Scots, who had generally come to take up the better, skilled jobs? Or the Asians in the West End and elsewhere? The Jews in Gateshead, the Arabs in South Shields?

There had always been newcomers, she replied. The point was the vast majority of people everywhere, the inner core, were the descendants of the original inhabitants, the original stock. They lived on as the same people. She had lost me there.

"Yes, we are aware of her expertise in that field. In fact it's that expertise we are particularly interested in."

This from the sergeant, in a Geordie lilt.

"Well if you knew that, why did you ask?"

"We'll ask the questions if you don't mind, sir. Please restrict yourself to answering them," ordered the inspector.

How could they possibly know that, if they didn't already know she was missing? Why not tell me that right at the beginning? Was I some kind of suspect all of a sudden? Then it dawned on me that of course I was. Woman goes missing: where does the finger of suspicion point straight away?

"I clearly am not the first person to have reported her missing, then."

"No sir," the inspector told me. "The lady at the supply agency, Miss Diane Weetwood – apparently an old friend of Miss Rorting – was surprised when she couldn't get in touch either by normal phone or mobile."

"And she kept on trying three days in a row, because she had another contract for a field-trip to Lordenshaw. The Willington Quay First School's history teacher, a Miss ..." he consulted his notes "... Moncur was apparently so impressed by Miss

Rorting that she recommended her to her colleague Mr Harvey at the Gallowgate First School."

"Well why didn't you tell me this right away?"

That was, of course, a very stupid question. And hadn't they just told me to stop asking questions? But why were they treating me like this?

Sensing the rising tension, Doctor Ingram interjected, "Tell me, Doctor Law, you said earlier that in the course of her educational work Miss Rorting was very good at acting out the parts of characters from history, or even prehistory? Do you think this sometimes extended into her everyday life?"

Funny he's asking that, when just a few moments ago I was myself remembering how she'd lost me with her talk about the original inhabitants living on as the same people. Then there are her dreams about living in the past, and the strange languages she seems to know. I don't know why really, because he's here to help, you'd think, but somehow I find myself on the defensive and reluctant to tell him the whole story. Best to try to laugh this last question off, I think.

"Well, she sometimes comes out with things that make you think that she's living in the past! She hates the Romans for instance! You should have seen her the time we visited the Museum of Antiquities at the university, when she started ranting at the professor there."

"That's very interesting, Doctor Law. Thank you for your answer. It's as if she were living another life, would you not say?"

I had no time to respond, but not because he did not give me the time. No, it was because my mind was working too sluggishly to think up anything that I might have wished to say.

He went on, "I note that you talk about Miss Rorting in the present tense. You clearly believe that she is still alive?"

"Of course I do," I snapped back, "I just want to know where she's got to. I want her back." This time, it all came blurting out without thinking.

"What exactly," the detective inspector began in the unmistakable tone of the interrogator to the suspect, "is the nature of your relationship with Miss Rorting?"

"We're neighbours, and very good friends."

"And lovers?"

I can't deny it, and why should I anyway?

"Yes."

Thirty seconds of silence and a few less reckless sips of the now cold coffee.

"And her moods, Doctor Law, would you say she's a moody person?" Ingram asked.

What was he getting at? What should I say? This latest question confirmed to me that the psychologist wasn't interested in me, he was there because of Linn. I thought back to the last day that I saw her, when she had come over all bubbly and had suddenly decided she wanted to take a trip to

Norway, when the day before she'd been sullen and depressed. And then I recalled the public screaming match she'd had with the piper, and then the evening we first met when she took up with me so quickly. I decided I'd try to make light of it. A bit of sexism, that might go down well with this bunch. I don't care what they think of me.

"She's a woman, isn't she? Par for the course, I'd say! Mind, she's a lot less moody than some I could mention, though but. And when you see what a stunner she is, you can forgive a lot."

"Doctor Law, I don't think you are taking this seriously enough. Do you realise we are trying to help your friend, and you?" said Ingram.

That's me put in my place, then! And he's right, really. The whole purpose of coming here was to ask them to help find Linn, so I need to tell them all I know... without getting myself locked up, if that's what they're bent on. Pull yourself together, Dodd, and answer all their questions! In detail. Even if you don't like these people, or the way they're going about their work.

"Sorry, I am doing my best, but I don't understand why you are asking some of these questions," I apologised, "Please, go on."

"So... Lordenshaw is famous for, amongst other things," the sergeant had to consult his notes again, "rock art, especially cup and ring art, isn't it?"

"I believe so... I mean yes, it is. Of course it is."

"Know a lot about that sort of thing, do we?"

He actually said "we".

"Well I know a little, yes. It was through our common interest in local history that we got... to become friends. And we both play the Northumbrian pipes. That is to say, she plays them very well and I am a rank beginner."

"And the last time you saw Miss Rorting? Did you part on good terms, would you say?"

"Actually, no. You might say she dumped me. For a student. We'd had a bit of a row – more like a tiff, really. About a rock. We lost it somehow."

"A rock?"

"Yes, a rock. I know it sounds odd. But it was special. And I don't know why, but it made Linn go. The rock. And that bloody student."

***

"I'll just make use of the gents' before I go, if you don't mind."

I stumbled as I asked the constable who had escorted me down the dingy corridor to the station exit.

"Be our guest, sir! I'll leave you here, then. Have a good afternoon."

They'd let me out after a lot more questions. They had to. It wasn't as if they had any reason to detain me, even if they had made me feel as if they did. But my head was spinning and my legs were weak and I just needed to sit down for a couple of minutes. Just after I'd locked myself into one of the

14

stalls, the entrance door swung noisily open. Two pairs of footsteps - one marching and one shuffling towards the urinals.

One of them broke wind, letting off the pent-up pressure with a dry, rasping sound.

"Oh, pardon me, inspector." It was Ingram!

"It was a long interview, I suppose. Thanks for holding it back till now! It would have changed the atmosphere for Mr Law," replied Breamish.

"Yes, in more ways than one, " Ingram admitted.

"Well, at least we now know the identity of the mystery friend that Miss Weetwood was worried about."

"Yes, but I don't think he knows anything that we didn't already know ourselves from our earlier talk with Miss Weetwood. And as far as Miss Rorting is concerned, he appears to have no inkling of her possible psychosis," replied Ingram.

Psychosis? Is that what he thinks? And what does he really mean by that anyway? Between the two of us, Miss Weetwood and I must have said something to raise his suspicions. They get on your nerves, these people, drawing sweeping conclusions based on a few questions. Well I for one will have none of it. She's fine to me. Spontaneous. Passionate. Committed... hang on, no, that's got a double meaning, hasn't it? Determined, then. A bit special, yes. But fine.

The Inspector went on: "I think it worked better with you sitting in with us, sir, rather than observing from behind the screen. He would have suspected something was up if just me and the Sergeant had gone through all those questions again."

"Yes, we should try it more often. It's an interesting case all round. Professionally speaking, I'd very much like to meet Miss Rorting. She sounds like a fascinating case to study in greater depth. I sincerely hope that nothing has befallen her. But I really think that if something has indeed happened to Miss Rorting, Mr. Law has got nothing to do with it."

"And how can you be so sure, Doctor Ingram?"

"Two things: the constancy of his gestures, and the consistent level of detail that he felt able to divulge. When someone's withholding information or lying, you can see their gestures unconsciously changing. Sometimes when I'm playing back a video of an interview, I turn down the sound and just concentrate on the gestures and I note the time when they change. Locking out the verbal stimuli helps me to focus on the movement of the hands, the shifting of position, the facial expression. Then I rewind back to just before the time I've noted, turn up the sound, and invariably it works - the next thing they say is a lie or a deliberate omission or evasion."

"That's interesting, sir. I'll give that a try myself. And the level of detail? You said that helps you too?"

Howay, man, get a move on! I'm stuck in here till they go, otherwise it's going to get very embarrassing.

"Why yes, most certainly. When someone wants to avoid describing a certain moment, they often go into elaborate details about events leading up to that moment and events after. It's a sure sign. Going back to Mr. Law, he was remarkably consistent in both respects. I am quite sure that he doesn't have a clue about how or why his mistress has disappeared, and he came in here this morning simply because he wants you to find her. Miss Weetwood had her suspicions about him because she doesn't know him. She just heard about him from Miss Rorting. But he's harmless. He doesn't have a clue."

Well, thank you very much for your confidently low opinion of my brain powers, Mr. Ingram. Hurry up, will you? Have you not finished yet?

Footsteps! Heading for the exit, I hope.

"So this Miss Rorting seems to be a complicated lady, sir. A strange mixture of repetitive, obsessive behaviour combined with impulsive and erratic moments, and unexplained absences. A psychotic, you say. And I say a bit of a mystery."

"Yes indeed, Inspector. So what do you…"

Their conversation was cut off by the creaking of the door as it closed behind them. At last! Though I'd like to have heard the rest of what they were saying.

I've had enough of this. I'm going up to Lordenshaw.

CHAPTER TWO – LORDENSHAW

There's a feeling you sense here on Lordenshaw which draws you back. Today more than ever. Standing on the limits of the Simonside hills with their sandstone ridges and rocky crags set out before your gaze. Timeless, as if they've never changed. Your nostrils quiver like the rabbits' around you with the intermingled pollens and scents of wild thyme, cranberry and cotton grass, bracken and ferns, and the purple blossom on the Northumberland heather. And the sap released from the juicy wild grass newly severed by the grazing sheep. Your boots sink into the yielding turf as you shift your stance to keep your balance and rest your palm onto the grassy slopes to steady your path as you explore the gullies and trenches of the ancient hill-fort.

There's silence all around, sometimes broken by what you imagine may have been the fluttering wings of a red grouse or a pheasant breaking cover, or footsteps on the rocks, or strides brushing through the heather, or voices on the wind. But when you turn to look, you can't quite make out the source. So you too feel released to shout at the top of your voice, or even practise your smallpipes, safe in the belief that no one will hear you. Or at least that if they do, you won't hear them complain.

Your throat gulps down the chill, windblown air gusting now up the slopes of the Coquet valley to the north, now over the outcrops to the south, now across the North Sea coastal plains to the east, and down from the old volcanic Cheviots to the north-west. Your whole body is buffeted as you lean forwards, backwards, sideways into the omni- and ever-present winds.

But still it's a calm that you feel. A feeling of being at home, as if you've known it all your life, and longer.

All the senses of your body tell you something about the place, but there's something extra that you can't quite describe. A calm which melds your senses together. As if you can reach out and touch the buzz of the insects, taste the shimmering hues of the flowers scattered wild in the fields, and see streams of musical notes floating past on the breeze. And I swear sometimes you can hear strange old voices, but when you turn, it's nothing but the heather growing. It's the heady effect of the Lordenshaw drug.

Was it this that drew our ancestors here who knows when, maybe six thousand years ago? Why didn't they choose a sheltered place, down in the valley on the banks of the Coquet? Even now it harbours some of the finest fishing pools in the world, so just imagine what it must have been like back then. What was the attraction of settling on top of an exposed hill, apart from the defensive possibilities? Or was that what preoccupied their different minds in those far-off days? And what was it like here in the dark of the night? What kind of people were they and whatever became of them? How did they cope with the force of a gale, a sodden downpour, or a blanket of snow? And why did they spend time, and how much time, carving the swirling, geometric patterns known today as cup and ring markings into the rocky outcrops and exposed boulders?

I would be almost unique among all its visitors if I hadn't stood on top of Lordenshaw and wondered. A chance happening up here one day inspired me to go beyond just wondering, and eventually brought me to this pretty pass.

***

It all began at Easter. It was quite late this year – the seventeenth of April. It was a clear and sunny early spring day, ideal for a hike up to the hill-fort. There aren't many days when the sun beats the wind chill and you can spread your thornproof on the rock, sit down in your shirt sleeves, and contemplate the view and the passing of time. The visibility was as good as it ever gets and I don't know if it was my imagination, but it seemed to me that I could make out the flecks of waves on the sea in the distance.

The air was soundless and pure and it was as if anyone from here to the horizon would be perfectly able to see and hear what I had in mind. But I'd been building up to this and now was the chosen time. I felt almost guilty as I looked all around, but there was not a soul in sight. I unzipped my pouch and felt inside for the velvety sac of skin. I drew it out, and under my rhythmic squeezing and coaxing, it steadily swelled up to its full, bloated size. Anybody overhearing the moans and groans would have wondered what was going on. So imagine my embarrassment when I looked up and realised that I was being watched from a short distance, just as I manhandled the groans and drones into a strangled version of a beginner's reel. I could hardly stop now, so I pressed on with my unconvincing and faltering rendition under the cool, appraising gaze of a tousle-haired, athletic-looking young woman. I self-consciously mouthed a greeting, trying, unsuccessfully I'm sure, to give the impression that I was well used to playing to an audience, however small.

As I ploughed dutifully on, she prowled watchfully in her simple drab-brown woollen tunic. Her languid strides parted the calf-high undergrowth, leaving tracks of dew and stains of pollen on her bare limbs. The bark of a retriever diverted her attention and, with a sudden start, she took to her heels and darted off with the dog in pursuit. Leaping and bounding, they gathered pace, as did my fingers on the chanter, and they were both out of sight over the brow of the ridge before I brought the reel racing to a conclusion. It was not the best of open-air débuts, and I resolved to take a few more lessons before venturing out in public again.

I scrambled up and over to the ridge to try to find her again, but she was nowhere to be seen. Only the dog was there, sniffing after the trail of a rabbit. I returned to the stone panel where I'd left my smallpipes, and gently packed them back into the gamekeeper's pouch across the lower back of my jacket. In so doing I noticed that my weight had embossed a facsimile of one of the cup and ring marks from the rock into the stiff, oiled cotton material. For an instant, I made to even it out but something changed my mind and I decided I liked it and that I'd leave it there and see how long it would last.

On my way back down the hill to the car park, I was disturbed to see that the passenger door of my car was open. Maybe I'd absentmindedly left it open in getting my pipes ready for their first outing on the hill - it certainly wasn't as if anyone would have spotted anything to steal from my old heap. The windows were so dirty, you could hardly see in anyway. A lady had the retriever from up on the hill on a leash and was leaning over the open door of the car.

"Ah, young man," she said. "I was thinking it was probably your car. I saw you up on the hill sitting on the big rock covered with cup and ring marks when I was looking for my dog, though I didn't care to go too near at the time..." - she shot me a meaningful glance – "and that you'd be down shortly, err... once you'd finished... I was just looking around to see if I could find the logbook in case I was going to have to report it to the police. It is your car then," she asked, taking another look at the logbook as she handed it over, "and you are Mr Dodd Law?"

"Yes, that's me and this is my car, such as it is. Thanks for taking the trouble to look after it."

"I was worried when I saw it - a car with its door wide open and looking abandoned."

"I can see how you thought it might have been abandoned! I haven't washed it for weeks, what with all the bad weather and all the mud I've been driving through recently. Today's the first decent day we've had in a good while, isn't it? But I'm surprised I actually left the door wide ajar. I must be doting."

"Well, even out here in the peace and quiet, you still need to be careful. Things can go astray and never be found again."

"Yes, thanks again. It was very kind of you. By the way, it sounds like you maybe know something about the cup and ring marks on the rocks?"

"Well, you know around these parts there are lots of old stories and superstitions, and not just about the cups and rings. Warlocks, fairies, elves, boggles - that's our name for ghosts, you know - all manner of strange creatures and spirits. In my family they used to say that the fairies made the cup holes with tiny picks that they stole from the miller. Then they used the cup holes to cool their porridge in!"

"I love these old stories. Luckily the fairies must have eaten the porridge before I got here today, because I sat right on top of one of the cup and ring markings. Look - you can see it's left a lasting impression on my coat!"

"Aye, I think you were too late for their breakfast time!"

"Maybe another day, then. Anyway. I noticed your dog was certainly enjoying himself, dashing around with your daughter... I suppose it was your daughter?"

"Oh, she so loves to chase around in the heather, does Nellie."

"Mind, that's an old-fashioned name for a girl."

"No, Nell's my dog. I was up there alone. My daughter is too old for gallivanting in the hills! Just me and young Nell here out for our morning walk."

"That's funny, because there was another younger woman playing with the dog. I even said hello to her. She must still be up there, I suppose."

"I suppose she must be. Maybe that's why Nell dashed off. Anyway, I need to be getting off now. I hope you enjoy the rest of your day out."

"Thanks very much. And you too. I thought I'd go for a run along some of the red-top roads out this way."

"Aye, it'll make you feel like king for the day!"

"How do you mean?"

"Why, don't you know? It's the same red road surface that the Queen and Prince Philip drive on when they parade along the Mall. You can't get it from anywhere else but just a few miles away from here, at the Biddlestone quarry."

"Well if it's good enough for those two, it's good enough for me! And if I may say so, the setting out here is far better than the Mall. Anyway, thanks again for looking after my car. Maybe see you here again some time."

"Well we're often here. It's champion for a good bracing walk. Good day to you."

"And to you, and Nell!"

Very strange that. Me leaving my car open. Feeling a bit guilty for the second time that day - she seemed to be a very nice lady - I found myself hunting around the car to see if anything was missing, but all seemed to be in its place. I decided to head through to Elsdon, past Winter's Gibbet and over to Otterburn to have a nice pub meal. Roast lamb, bread-and-butter pudding, and a couple of pints of seventy shillings and I'd be back in fine fettle!

CHAPTER THREE –A QUEST BEGINS

I looked down at the fading imprint of the symbol on my coat and compared it with the image on the website. Yes, that's the one. And that's the rock I was sitting on, and they've even got its exact Ordnance Survey longitude and latitude, measured by GPS. The Internet certainly is a wonderful thing for researching into any subject under the sun. Except when you get interrupted by a power cut. Another oil crisis, I heard on the Mike Neville Show. At least I'd been in time to download myself some of that artificial intelligence that you hear about to remedy some of my real ignorance.

Well, what have I learnt this morning? For a start, things seem to be a lot less clear-cut than when they taught me about history way back when in my school Stone Age. We learnt that history was largely a series of invasions and battles where successive new tribes came along and swept away the poor unsuspecting natives, who'd done precisely the same thing to some other poor beggars the century before. It always seemed as if the changeovers happened overnight, and the losers just disappeared out of sight. Now I'm learning that everything happened a lot more subtly and gradually, and for the most part much less dramatically.

No one's really sure when the first rock carvings were made here, but it seems like the first ones appeared towards the end of the New Stone Age. It means that our ancestors had already settled down long enough to put down some roots and make their mark on the rocks of Lordenshaw and other hills and moorland around here.

The cup and ring markings from Northumbria are pretty much unique in England. You don't find them in the midlands or south, and there are only very few localities in Europe which have anything like them. Northumbria of course means the land north of the Humber, extending through modern North Yorkshire and Durham, to the north of Northumberland and the Scottish borders. The markings got their name some time in the second half of the nineteenth century because people thought the hole in the middle looked a bit like a cup, and then you've got circles cut into the rock around the cup. Quite often there's a kind of gutter running out from the cup and through the rings.

No one knows what the markings mean or what they were for. There are lots of different ideas: ranging from practical ones like they could have been Stone Age signposts or maps, to spiritual ones suggesting they could have been religious symbols. It's a mystery, and what's more it's our very own Northumbrian mystery, which I kind of like the sound of. A Geordie mystery: that suits me down to the ground. This could be the makings of another good hobby – I'm at a bit of a loose end anyway, what with having just got back to the region after too long away. Taking up the smallpipes was, I suppose, part of the same symptoms of longing for home which eventually brought me back to where I belong.

Going away in the first place had been a take-it-or-leave-it decision anyway. It had been the last thing on my mind when it happened. There I was, just out of university and straight into a lab job in a spanking new, giant electronics factory. It had been set up only a couple of months earlier near the Coast Road by a German multi-national on the back of major government aid to entice inward investment into the North-East.

No sooner had I finished the induction-training course and got to grips with my first assignment in the production engineering unit than the HQ announced that the factory was going to be mothballed. They cited 'unforeseen, highly unfavourable changes in market conditions'. Apparently, customers could all of a sudden buy equivalent products at less than a quarter of the price in the Far East. If it had been so unforeseen to them, they must have been not only short-sighted, but blind.

To cut a long story short, I'd been one of the few lucky ones without too many ties, and with the stipulated working knowledge of German. All of us willing and able to take up the company's consolation-prize offer of a short-term contract at a new factory they were setting up in the old East Germany. Building a new generation of the devices they said they couldn't afford to build on Tyneside. Some irony there. I misguidedly thought it was going to be in Frankfurt, the bustling economic capital. But when I got off the company-chartered plane along with the few colleagues who'd also taken up this lifeline, we found ourselves in the other Frankfurt, an der Oder, the run-down town on the Polish border. The gleaming city, Frankfurt Am Main, it most assuredly was not. They put us up in a barely refurbished old Communist housing block. Despite the rough conditions, me and me marras had a whale of a time.

The wages were nothing like they would have been in the 'real' Frankfurt, but life was cheap out in the wasteland, and we could send money home, put some aside for the inevitable rainy day when our contracts would run out, and still have enough to throw around on wine, women and song, or should I say *Bier, Fräuleins und Oompah.* The demands of our work and play environments where everyone spoke German, or if pushed, Russian, ensured that we were soon more or less operational in Krautspeak, making us trilingual when you added in English and Geordie. This turned us into fairly marketable propositions and

when we saw the writing on the wall for our
temporary contracts, we found it not too difficult
to fix ourselves up with new jobs before we got the
push. I plumped for the other Frankfurt this time,
and doubled my salary, even though I was still
earning less than the locals. The lure of the lucre
became my guiding light, anything to swell my
coffers, and I chopped and changed my way
through ever more lucrative jobs around northern
Europe over the next few years. I ended up in
Hilversum, of 'funny name on an old radio dial'
fame.

And that's where I had what seemed initially to
be the good fortune, but latterly turned out to be
the gross misfortune to get involved with Fanny. A
drunken night in Groningen had brought us
together, and we almost literally fell in with each
other. When she told me that Groningen was
twinned with Newcastle, my fate was sealed.
There were moments in the first year when she
really did light my life up, but a few rocky months
towards the end of the second year managed to
douse any ardour I had left.

The trouble was, I could see something of the
person I had become over the last few years in all
of them, and I didn't much care for what I saw.
Too materialistic. Too driven. No time or
inclination to sit and wonder. Or just sit. One day I
found myself joining in with her family and
drinking from a communal bucket that they filled
up from the windscreen washer tap at the
motorway services. Talk about tight. I just found
myself on the edge of it all and asking myself how

did I end up with this bunch, and did I really want to be there? What was I doing with my life? And could I see myself doing this for the foreseeable future? And the answers were, 'it wasn't my idea', 'no', 'nothing', and 'no'. I needed something for the soul, some uncertainty, some entropy. I needed to be in a place I felt a part of, and this was not the place. It was time to get out.

When I heard on the grapevine about a good job going begging back home, it was a ready-made way out of this predicament. And the prospect of splitting up from the madwoman from Makkum, a small town near Heerenveen in Holland, gave me a good push in a northerly direction too.

Which reminds me. I wonder who she was, that so still, and then suddenly so wild-running girl up on the hill yesterday? The memory of her appearance, and disappearance, troubles me. But seeing the illustrations on the prehistoric rock-art websites, she looked as if she would have fitted in very well with the people of the time. I don't suppose I'll see her again.

CHAPTER FOUR – NORTHUMBRIAN PIPES LESSON

There she is! I don't believe it. Coincidences like this don't happen in real life. Or do they?

"Hello. It might be a strange question, but didn't I see you up in the hills near Rothbury a few days ago? At Lordenshaw, where the Iron Age hill-fort is."

"You might have. It's one of my favourite places. I sometimes go fell-running there. And it's to do with my work. I'm involved in local history and conservation, so I know a fair bit about the hill-fort and the rock-carvings up there."

She spoke not with a Tyneside accent, but with a Northumbrian burr, the characteristic uvular 'rrr' coming from the back of her throat rather than from the trilling of her tongue. Like Harry Hotspur in Shakespeare's King Henry IV, Part One. It sounded wonderful, and I just wanted to hear her talk some more.

"I said hello but you didn't seem to notice."

"That could just be me. Dreaming. When I'm up there, it's as if I get spirited away. If it was me, I'm sorry."

"Maybe I didn't say it loud enough… I was playing the pipes."

"Now I think I would have noticed that! Anyway what brings you to the Sage?"

"Well in case you're wondering, I'm not here to see that Abba tribute band from Gateshead."

"Oh, you mean Shmabba?"

"Aye, that's them, the ones that do 'Shekels, Shekels, Shekels'."

"You like them really, don't you?"

"Yes, I admit it! But actually I'm here to learn. That's my inspiration over there, Billy Pigg. The Border Minstrel was what they called him. He was probably the finest Northumbrian pipes player that's ever lived. It's a good photo they've got of him – the same one as on the old record of his music that I've got. Him, and in the modern era, Kathryn Tickell. There's a beginners' lesson on tonight, and that's why I'm here wrestling with these smallpipes. I love these music rooms down here in the basement. You can go in, shut the door, and blast away. I don't dare practise in the apartment where I live – I'm bad enough anyway, and they make quite a noise, even if they're a whole lot quieter than Scottish bagpipes."

"Oh aye, the GBH! Not a patch on the Northumbrian pipes. I have the same problem with the noise when I'm practising too. I'm a player myself, and I'm going to be performing at your session. Look, I've got my pipes here too."

"Mind, they're complicated ones, aren't they? Mine are a basic set in F+, with a seven-key chanter, though I haven't really progressed onto using the keys yet. I'm quite happy staying within my own little octave at the moment. Which I can't really do anyway!"

"I've been through a few different sets over the years. These are just about the most complete you can get, with a seventeen-key chanter and set of drones all in African blackwood. These allow me to play two full octaves, plus I've got tuning beads on each drone."

"You make them sound like a hot-rod – you know, like 'A sixty-nine Chevy with a three-ninety-six, fuelie heads and a Hurst on the floor'."

"Well, I suppose to me, that's what they are. Something I can tinker with - try to make perfect. Where did you get that from, those words? They sound familiar."

"Oh, it's an old song, 'Racing in the streets'. You could look it up on iTunes, or LimeWire, if you're that way inclined. My dad used to play it to us in the car."

"Thanks, I might do. Anyway this set, this hot-rod of mine, gives me the space to play more easily with other instruments because they're in G, which is good for ensemble work. Though it means the finger-holes are spaced very close together. Luckily I've got slender hands."

"They look beautiful... Your pipes, I mean. Err, and your hands, of course. Both of them. Or rather, all three. Your pipes and your two hands. If you see what I mean."

"Why, thank you for that two-handed compliment! Aye, they are nice. I'm proud of them. And so they should be. For the price. A thousand pounds, these cost!"

"My God! Those manicurists are raking it in with people like you around! No, but really, you must be mad keen on playing!"

"I am. I play them daily. And it's a craftsman's work to produce a set like these, you know. A labour of love. And when you see the time and skill that goes into making them, you can understand why the price is what it is."

"I'm just hiring mine for the present to see how I get on, before I splash out a few hundred quid on a simpler set like these. The biggest difficulty I'm having is getting used to the fingering. I used to play the recorder at school, so I've got it built-in to lift off a row of fingers at a time. Now I've got to get used to just taking off one finger to sound a note. And then there are the keys... and then there's trying to keep a level pressure coming out of the bag... it's what your left elbow's for, as they say... the list goes on. Though I'm enjoying it, very much. I feel it brings me back in touch with the region."

"So you've been away?"

"Aye, ten years. In Europe. On the continent. I've come back here to work and my employer found me a place to rent. Just across the river from here."

"I live just across the river too. That's how I can pop across the Millennium Bridge and play down in these music rooms too."

"So you mean you live close?"

"Aye, I've got a place overlooking the river, Hanover Lofts."

"That really is amazing, mind, because that's where I've just moved. What a coincidence. Two pipers in the same building. Though maybe I shouldn't call myself a piper, more a bladder-strangler at the moment. There were a fair few empty places on the back at a not-bad rent so I'm staying there until I decide what to do. I'm really glad that they didn't pull them all down when they fell into disrepair, and after all of those fires that raged in them. It's lucky the fire brigade was so quick on the scene those three times they had the fires. In another life they would have been damaged beyond repair. That big, ugly, modern hotel that used to block the view from the warehouses wasn't so lucky though in the last fire, was it? Totally gutted. Too bad they had to knock it down. Which is great for our lofts of course, as it opens up the view of the river. Did you say you've got one with a view?"

"Yes, I'm lucky. Somehow my family owned a stretch of the Quayside and one of the conditions that I put to the developer was that I'd keep the top-floor loft for myself."

"Not bad! I had a look at one on the river side, but the price was way out of my league. Some fat cat's making a packet!"

"Hanover Street is a marvellous place, isn't it? Like stepping back into the past," she remarked, changing the subject. "In my mind, it's the best-preserved street in Newcastle. And still the most evocative of old times when the Quayside was a teeming mass of humanity come from the surrounding countryside and further afield, Scotland and Ireland and even the Nordic and Baltic countries, in search of work and better prospects. My ancestors were amongst them, living, or more like surviving, in the Entries and Heughs and Chares and Passages that ran up the banks away from the Quayside and off the Side and Sandhill. Even a packed Friday night now can't compete with the numbers of people who were crammed into the narrow passages back in the nineteenth-century boomtown. Though it's certainly better fun now."

"Aye," I joined in, "it's got history. That's why I really like it too. The entrance door to my apartment gives onto Hanover Street bank. The old uphill wagonway. The old setts of cobbles for the carthorses to grip on and the twin cast-ways of heavy pink Shap granite carriage-stones that the wheels ran on to pull the carts up the steep winding bank from the quay. For some reason, they only have them for the upward journey on the left side of the road. They mustn't have needed them for the downhill run. Someone said the idea originally came from hill roads in Northern Italy."

"And the giant street numbers above each of the warehouse entrances. I'm glad they preserved them when they did the old bonded warehouses up. It's the only such street left in the city. In fact it's nigh-on unique in England now."

"I'm in the block with the big green number forty on the wall. They had flats in all of them, numbers ten, twenty, thirty, forty and fifty. But there was something about number forty I liked. And you're right, there's something special about Hanover Street. We're so lucky it's so well preserved."

"You know the road and the buildings date from 1844 – you can see the stone date-plaques high up on the walls between the giant numbers. Seven storeys of Flemish bond brick. Truly magnificent."

"Hey look, they're calling us for the start of the lesson. Maybe we can walk back together after? My name's Dodd Law, by the way."

"Dodd Law? Did you have a friend called Ron with a sister a few years younger in the school over the road from yours?"

"Yes, I did. Ron Milburn. I still see him at the match now and then."

"I knew there was something about you! She was at least a couple of years above us, but when we used to look through the railings at all the sixth formers, she used to tell us your names. We thought you all looked so grown up and cool!"

"Not so cool now! Grown up yes, maybe, but cool... I think that's passed me and Ron by, by now!"

"Oh, I don't know... Anyway, I'm Linn Rorting. Pleased to know you, Dodd."

"And you, Linn. How about we meet up at the end and walk back over the bridge?"

"Fine! See you then."

During the lesson, Linn gave us a short recital, including a beautiful piece, a lament, which she repeated several times without it ever coming to a final resolution.

***

"What was that piece you played for us, Linn? I have the feeling I've heard it before," I asked as we walked back.

"I don't think you could have heard it. Unless the music-room walls here are thinner than I thought they were. It's my own piece. I feel as if I've been working on it forever. But I can never get to the end."

We were just approaching the middle of the Millennium Bridge.

"Linn, I've got an idea. Were you here on the opening night of the bridge? You know, when Kathryn Tickell stood where we are right now and played a long piece she'd written specially for the occasion?"

"I was, aye! It was quite a night. Getting a certificate for being one of the first thousand to cross the bridge. And I loved her piece – the way she built it. 'Music for a new crossing', that's what it's called."

"Well, could you play your lament here? It might help you to find the missing ending. Howay man, before another herd of stags or clutch of chicks gets onto the bridge. Gan on, give it a try. Please!"

"Err... oh, all right. Why not? I've always wanted to do it, to tell the truth. As long as you accompany me. Try to follow the changes – I'll give you the nod. Mind, it'll be tricky, what with your pipes being in F+. But just back off the pressure a bit and that should bring you down to around nonplussed F. Then try to find a few notes that will work as a simple accompaniment."

To say the least, I was nonplussed at these quick instructions, but there was no going back!

We set ourselves looking up river over the reflected lights of the Millennium Bridge itself towards the Tyne Bridge, the Swing Bridge, the High Level, the Edward VII and Metro rail bridges, and the Redheugh Bridge beyond. Linn started slowly but upped the tempo as she grew in confidence, while I stayed in the background with little more than a drone and tried not to put Linn off with too many hesitations in the changes. A few passers-by stopped to listen and even dropped a few coppers into Linn's sack!

But then I noticed some blue flashing lights on the Gateshead side coming along from the Swing Bridge.

"Linn, I think we'd better stop! You probably need a licence or something to do this, especially if people start giving us money!"

"But I still haven't worked out the ending!"

"Howay man, let's go!"

We picked up our bags and hurried away, our takings jingling away in Linn's bag. We started to run as we gathered speed on the steepening slope at the end of the footbridge and kept up the pace as we ran all along the Quayside, darting and dodging between the straggling groups of late-night stag and hen parties, slow-cruising white stretch limousines, and high-spirited lads and lasses. Some of the lads and even some of the lasses made half-hearted and heavy-limbed attempts to rugby-tackle us. But this is a football town, so they missed. We raced along under the Tyne Bridge, not daring to look skywards as we bobbed and weaved for fear of being bombed by the nesting kittiwakes and gulped in the acrid guano-laden air. Then it was round the Guildhall, and on to the home stretch past Bettie Surtees' house and Julie's and the Cooperage and on non-stop to Linn's entrance to Hanover Lofts. She certainly could run. Racing in the streets.

"Hey, you're a good runner, Dodd!"

"Actually, I'm training for the Great North Run. It's one of those things I've always wanted to do. And with being back in the region – being back home is what I really mean – I thought it would be a great way to get off on the right foot."

"Another coincidence! Can you believe this? This year will be my fifth Great North Run. Two runners and two pipers – or hey, what about two running pipes players? – living in the same block of flats!"

"Aye, two drips, tappy-lappying alang! I hope you're not proposing to do the Run playing the pipes, are you?"

"No, 'course not. But mind, you see a lot stranger sights than that, I can tell you. Last year I passed a monk running together with Adolf Hitler. And to make it even funnier, they were both eating ice-creams from that cockney mackem ice-cream man on the John Reed Road. And that night I saw them being interviewed on Tyne Tees. They said they'd trained hard all year, eating at least five ice-creams a week."

"There are certainly some, well, interesting characters around, aren't there? But hang on, if this year's your fifth, that means you must have done your first when you were, what, sixteen? As soon as you reached the minimum age?"

"Hee, hee ... and the rest."

It was a nice try, I thought, but there was no way she was giving her age away. But from what she'd said, I reckoned she really couldn't be more than twenty-seven or -eight.

"We could run together," Linn suggested, "and I promise you won't have to play the pipes as we run."

"Well, we could certainly start together, but you'll soon leave me behind."

Even as I was saying this, I was remembering the view I'd had of her hockey-girl calves glowing pink from the exertion of the run as I'd trailed along in her wake, and thinking what a great excuse even the training would be to spend some time together.

"But hey, yeah, that would be fantastic, let's do – or at least start - the Run together."

"It's a deal. Mind, we'll have to do some training together as well."

Is she reading my mind, I wondered. I hope not, as lustful thoughts of those glistening calves re-surfaced.

"Listen," she continued, as if still on exactly the same subject, "I'm taking a couple of school classes for a field-trip into the hills on Friday morning. Why don't you come along? I was just going to do the usual local history, flora and fauna, but why don't we give it a theme of cup and ring markings and hill-forts and go up to Lordenshaw?"

"Sounds great. I'll see if I can re-arrange things at work to be able to come."

"If you can make it, drop a note in my letterbox here, and I'll get back in touch with the details of where to meet. See ya!"

And she was gone, just like that. She was a live wire all right – and, as I was beginning to admit to myself, a quite adorable one to boot. Was she always this bubbly and go-getting, or was this the top end of some manic curve? It struck me that coincidence was one thing, but fate quite another.

CHAPTER FIVE – THE FIELD-TRIP

"Good morning to you all, the children of Saint Aidan's School, Willington Quay and Wylam County Primary School. And to your teachers, Miss Moncur and Miss Heslop."

"Good morning, Miss!"

"My name's Linn Rorting and I'm a local historian and a naturalist."

"Eeeh, Miss, doesn't that mean you go round with no clothes on?"

"You're thinking of a naturist, boy," admonished Miss Heslop from Wylam.

"I certainly am!"

"No, actually it means I'm interested in the conservation of the wildlife and the countryside as well as the ancient history of Northumbria. Now I only got to know a couple of days ago that I'd be taking classes from Willington Quay and Wylam, and as well as the ancient history of Northumberland I am also very interested in the area's more recent, industrial history. And in terms of industrial history there is something very special that links your two towns. Does anyone know what that is?"

"They're both on the river Tyne, Miss. A knaa that, Miss, coz me daa took iz fishin up Wylam way. An Will'n Quay's defnitly on the Tyne, coz Aa cin see it from me bedroom winda."

Plenty of giggles, especially from the Wylam side.

"There's nothing to laugh at, nothing at all. In fact ... sorry, what's your name? Jimmy Sample? In fact Jimmy's hit the nail on the head, Willington Quay and Wylam are both on the Tyne, and so our river definitely does link the two. And because of the river and the coalfield, a very special local figure - a local hero, really - began to dabble in steam power and steam engines."

A raising of arms, clicking fingers, and hissings of Miss, Miss.

"Please Miss, it was George Stephenson, wasn't it? He came from Wylam, but he moved to Will'n Quay later and his son Robert was born there. And Miss, there's anotha junya school in Will'n Quay, and it's caalled the George Stephenson sumthin, er, Memorial Aa think, aye the George Stephenson Memorial School. But everybody just caals it the Stivvies rund wor way like, Miss."

More Wylam laughter.

"That's absolutely right... Jimmy ... so you can all be very proud indeed of the towns you come from, and you'll be able to find all sorts of traces of their past if you just look around a little. Old railway lines leading from the pits down to the Tyne for example. George worked on stationary engines that hauled the coal trucks, and then he went on to perfect a locomotive. He didn't actually invent the railway locomotive, but he made the first one that worked properly and was really reliable. It was called..."

About twenty kids in unison: "The Rocket, Miss!"

"That's right! Very good! And Robert also went on to be a great builder of locomotives, and had a very important works behind the Central Station in Newcastle, in South Street, not far from where I live. There's only one surviving building from Stephenson's factory now, one of the old machine rooms. It now contains a small museum, which is well worth a visit."

"George also invented a special safety lamp for miners. You can see an example donated by George in the Lit and Phil Society at the bottom end of Westgate Road, where he first demonstrated his invention, just along from the station. It's got a marvellous library, including lots of children's books and you know, anyone can join. George's invention was a great success and it became known as the Geordie lamp, and the miners in our area wouldn't use any other kind of lamp, and so they - and then all the people in the region - became known as the Geordies. So you can all be really proud of being Geordies."

"But now let's move even further back in time than the nineteenth century. A lot further back, in fact. You have probably been wondering why I brought you all up here to the top of this hill today, haven't you? Well, I am going to be your guide to Lordenshaw and its rock-carvings and Iron Age hill-fort."

"This curved, grassy bank that we're all standing on is the outer wall of the Iron Age hill-fort. The site is about a hundred and forty metres across. Every so often you can see some exposed stones of the wall, especially over there at the eastern gateway. If you peel away the thin layer of turf, you can also see the smooth rock slabs which made up the pathway into the fort. Further down that side of the hill, there are great expanses of smooth outcrop sandstone with faint cup and ring markings."

"We came in through the western entrance, which is on the path from the public car park. It's not so easy to make out where it was. On the inside of the wall, there's this nearly three-metre-deep ditch and then another lower bank, which is the inner wall. As you walk around inside the fort you'll see a few small circular dips in the ground, about five metres across, where they built their houses. Though actually some of those are probably from the later period after the Roman invasion, long after the walls and ditches were constructed."

"You can see we have a commanding view on all sides, so this would have been a perfect defensive position, if this really is why they built their settlement up here. If you look over there outside the fort on the north-east point of the hill, that's an ancient burial cairn which you can go and have a look at by yourselves later. Look carefully and you should be able to see some cup and ring markings on the outcrops of rock."

"Then look over the valley at the terraces cut into the slopes where ancient farmers worked. The climate in the Bronze and Iron Ages was probably a few degrees warmer than now, so good farming land was found even in upland places like the Simonsides, where now we only see moorland and these abandoned terraces. Though it seems that soil erosion also played a part after the hills were cleared of their forest cover and the land was cultivated, loosening the topsoil. So the first hill terracing was done in prehistoric times to combat the erosion and the soil being washed away by the rains."

"I'm going to give you a short talk on prehistoric times in this area of north Northumberland. I don't mind at all if you pipe up with questions or comments – it'll make it more fun for us all! The main thing is that you pay attention and learn something."

"So let's begin. Do you know that where we're standing used to be in the Southern Hemisphere, around about where the Falkland Islands are today? Yes, about five hundred million years ago, this was part of a land called Avalonia. The ancient Iapetus Ocean separated us from another continent called Laurentia, which included what we now call Scotland. Over the following hundred million years, during the same period that fish were evolving legs and coming out of the sea onto the land and the first seed-bearing plants were developing, the two continents crept towards each other, squeezing the Ocean away and bringing Scotland into collision with England. That is why the geology of the rocks here in Northumberland is completely different from Scotland - the rocks are from different continents."

"You can imagine the tremendous forces that must have been set up. The earth crumpled and was forced upwards to form the Caledonian mountain range and volcanic lava from the centre of the earth erupted along the collision line to create the Cheviots. The border between Scotland and Northumbria closely follows the border between ancient Avalonia and Laurentia. So our land of Northumbria has been a border not only for hundreds of years, but for hundreds of millions of years. We are standing in a very special place indeed."

"And where we are standing, Stone Age man once stood. Can anyone tell me what a Stone Age man is?"

"Yes, Miss! Me dad says it's a mackem!"

"Nah, it's someone like you, you duck-egg."

I hadn't heard anyone say that for years.

"Now, now! That's enough of that," said the class teachers in unison.

"Well Stone Age men are called that because the only tools they used were made out of things they found around them – stone, wood, bones, and so on. But because the first people lived such a long time ago, only the stones have survived."

"The first stone tools like on this photo were found in Ethiopia and come from about two and a half million years ago at the beginning of the Old Stone Age. They were just pebbles with the corners chipped or flaked away to sharpen them, as you can see here," said Linn, pointing at the poster.

"What's that 'p' word on the picture, Miss?"

"That's the Palaeolithic Age – which is Greek for the Old Stone Age, because in this age the stones were chipped or flaked away. In the New Stone Age, the stones were shaped by polishing too. We call that the Neolithic Age."

"They'll have used naturally sharp stones before then, but of course you can't tell which ones!"

"Bone, antlers and wood were also used, not just stone, but stones obviously lasted longer. The others we can't find so easily. As time went on they perfected the use of hand-axes, the pear-shaped ones that you see on cartoons like the Flintstones."

"Never heard of the Flintstones, Miss Rotten."

"Ror – ting, not Rotten!" corrected Miss Heslop, "and the Flintstones was a cartoon show when I was at school during the Stone Age, or at least I suppose that's what you all think."

"Thank you, Miss Heslop. One thing about real flints is that they make sparks when you strike them, and around about one and a half million years ago man learnt how to use fire to keep warm and eventually for cooking."

"The Old Stone Age lasted for more than two million years. Dare I say that progress was very slow? You could live your whole life and things wouldn't look any different from the day you were born! Not like nowadays, when one year it's the Spice Girls, the next it's Britney, and the next it's Beyoncé!"

"Who're the Spice Girls, Miss?"

"See what I mean? They must be from at least five years ago! Anyway, back to slower-moving times... Eventually we come to the Middle Stone Age which lasted from about 180,000 to 40,000 years ago. This was when they started to get a lot better at making hand-axes and also special pointed and scraper tools made out of flint. And around about then, Neanderthal man came along too."

"Aye, THAT would be the mackems! Sorry, Aa was wrong before."

"No, they are called Neanderthal man because remains of them were found in the Neander valley near Düsseldorf in Germany. You know, Düsseldorf, where the first Auf Wiedersehen Pet series was set... I know! Don't tell me. You've never heard of it! You must think I'm a boring old fart..."

Splutters, gurgles, and elbow digs.

"Eeeh, Miss!"

"Whoops, sorry, I was getting carried away! You've never heard of that either, have you? I'm getting old! Anyway, it was a really good comedy drama about builders from the North-East and other places who went out there to work. So there is a Geordie connection there, too. Perhaps the Neanderthalers had actually moved over from here to Germany looking for work." Plenty of giggles. This approach was working.

"Then we move into the Upper Stone Age. Who can remember the Greek word for Stone Age?"

"Summat Thick, Miss?"

"Aye, Geordie Thick."

"Mackem Thick, you mean."

"No, not quite."

"Anyone with a better memory?"

"Palaeolithic!"

"Yes! So now we're in the Upper Palaeolithic Age going from about 40,000 years ago to about 10,500 years ago. Humans by this time are physically like modern people, and they develop all sorts of specialised tools like spears, needles to sew with, knives, hammers, and axes. In fact it must have been like walking through a DIY store. This photo shows you a few examples."

"It was also in this age that we start to find examples of art and carvings on rocks and in caves."

"But before that, does anyone know another way of saying 10,500 years ago?"

"Come on, Saint Aidan's! You know this one," said Miss Moncur, encouraging her class.

"Miss, it's 8,500 BC, for Before Christ."

"Well done, Hedley."

"And that was the end of the last Ice Age. This was also the time of the New Stone Age, when they learnt how to polish and grind stone tools into shape, instead of chipping and flaking the edges off."

"The change in the climate changed the landscape and the animals too. Thick forests grew up everywhere and herds of wild cattle, maybe looking like the Chillingham white cattle on this photo, and horses and deer roamed all over, searching for the best grazing pastures. People had no choice but to follow them, so they lived like nomads, meaning people who moved around and didn't settle in one single place. People still live like that in the Sahara desert even now."

"And in Manchester, Miss. We went to a match, me cousin and me and me uncle, and we saw them all livin' in cardboard boxes in a square somewhere."

"Well, that's as may be. But let's press on. About 6,000 BC was a special time when the melting ice and the rising sea turned Britain into an island split apart from the continent. Before that you could walk straight across, no need for the Channel Tunnel or the ferry."

"Miss, does that mean there might be towns hidden under the sea?"

"Well maybe not towns, but certainly there would have been places where people lived, and if we were very good at guessing where to search, we could look under all the mud of the sea-bed and we'd find hand-axes and so on."

"By about 3,500 or 3,000 BC, people in Britain were establishing themselves into communities that were more complicated than just families living together. Some people decided they wanted to be in charge, depending on their strength or special skills or property, or knowledge of religions and beliefs."

"These communities began making their own mark on the landscape with organised and permanent places to live. And of course literally making their mark by carving the cup and ring markings into the rocks. And also building the first of the mysterious stone monuments and circles. Mind, you don't find these everywhere. You've all heard of Stonehenge, shown on this picture, haven't you? And maybe Avebury stone circle too? Both are down in the south of England and came a bit later, around about 2,300 to 2,000 BC. But have you heard of Castlerigg stone circle? Well, it really is not so far away from here. It's between Ullswater and Derwentwater in the Lake District, and was built much earlier, around 3,000 to 2,500 BC. Here's an aerial photo."

"Now, we don't have any of those standing-stone circles here in Northumberland. Though I tell a lie, we do have a few so-called four-posters where you have four standing stones arranged a bit like the four corners of a big four-poster bed. And there are some places with a few stones arranged in lines instead of circles. But we do have henges, for instance up on Milfield Basin, north of Wooler. A henge doesn't have to be made out of stone, you know. It's actually the circular ditch and wall that is called the henge. The ones up at Milfield had wooden posts around the henge instead of standing stones. If you have a chance, you should try to get up to see the wonderful reconstruction of a henge at the Maelmin Trail at Milfield."

"Many archaeologists now think that the special rock-carvings that we're going to see on this hill this afternoon were first done by the people around about the same period as those stone circles. And the funny thing is - we have the rock-carvings here but no stone circles, and the people who made stone circles didn't put rock-carvings on them. Now that's a mystery."

"Though maybe I should say that there is always an exception to prove the rule: if you ever go to see the four-poster standing stones called the Goatstones near Wark, you'll see that one of them does actually have cup markings on top. The question is, though, whether the marks had already been made generations before the standing stones were set up."

"Now I hope that after today, some of you are going to come back here or to some of our other beautiful hills and ancient sites up here in north

Northumberland. Have any of you ever been to any of the other hill-forts around here?"

"I've been up Yeavering Bell, Miss. It was even bigger than this, but it was a long hike from our car."

"Oh, that's wonderful. The biggest hill-fort in the area. I love walking around there too. It's like a twin hill, isn't it? A hill with twin peaks."

"Anyone else? No? Well, I hope some time you will do. I really would recommend Yeavering Bell, which is up near Wooler. It's very close to the Maelmin Trail and the Milfield Basin that I was telling you about just before. And at its foot, on a strange plateau in the valley below is Gefrin, the ancient seat of the Kings of Northumbria from the 600's AD, not BC. It grew to its peak in the time between when the Romans left and invaders like the Vikings started to arrive. Then you have wonderful moorland dotted with rocks covered with cup and ring markings at places between here and Wooler and beyond, such as Weetwood Moor, Kettley Crag, and Chatton Park. And you have other hill-forts at places like Humbleton Hill and Great Hetha. You're lucky to live so close, because our hill-forts are better preserved here in Northumberland than anywhere else in the British Isles. They're so remote and set out here in the wilds where there has been so little development of any kind."

"It's one of the effects of being a border region where over hundreds of years, development and investment was held back. No one could see the point in working on anything long-lasting or building anything permanent, when from one day to the next it could be ransacked or taken over by invaders from the north or even from the next valley in the time of the Reivers. But there I go, jumping ahead by a thousand years! We have so many ancient sites here that many have still never been excavated by archaeologists. Maybe if you're lucky, your schools can organise another trip next year so you can see some more. I'd love to come along too."

"Now, getting back to the stone circles like Stonehenge, some people think they are to do with rituals or mystical religions because they're often aligned with the mid-summer or mid-winter sun, and some people think our rock carvings might be too. And talking of circles, can anyone think of a really important invention that arrived here at about the same time?"

"No ideas? Well, let me tell you - it was the wheel. This must have made a huge difference to everyday life. The first wheel anyone has found was in Mesopotamia and goes back to four thousand and something BC. It probably reached us here in the three thousands BC. You can see the similarities between the wheel and the cup and ring markings, can't you?"

"Well, I think that's enough of me just talking! Now we're going to go and look at some of Northumberland's very own prehistoric art. Does anyone have any questions on what I've been saying?"

"Yes Miss, is he your boyfriend?"

The cheeky little urchin is pointing at me!

"No! I asked for questions about what I've been saying! And anyway, it's none of your business, little girl!"

"Look, he's gone all red. He is, isn't he?"

"Well, let's see if you have some other questions after you've done some work."

"You've all got the maps of the fort that I gave out? Well, I've got two tasks for you. Firstly, I want you to draw pictures of the most interesting things that you see and describe what you think they are. Keep a look out for the east and west entrances to the fort, the round dips in the ground where they built their houses, the burial cairns, the cup and ring markings on the rocks of course, and anything else you discover yourselves that you think might be archaeological evidence of how and where they lived. If you're really good explorers, you might even find the famous horseshoe rock with its mysterious carvings. It's hidden away not very far from here. You can go off and explore in any direction, even down the hill and onto the moorland, over to the old farming terraces on the other hills over there if you like, but don't go out of sight of your teachers."

"And secondly I'd like you to trace copies of some cup and ring markings and then make some guesses of what they were for. Like I told you, nobody knows why they made them, so one of you might come up with the answer that no one's ever thought of! Over the next week, I'm going to go through all of your work, and the best team is going to win a special prize."

"Now one last thing before we get started. I want to give you a very important safety instruction, so I need you all to look and listen carefully. I am going to show you something I have in my bag here. There! What's this?"

"A snake skin, Miss!"

"Yes. The skin of an adder, shed in the spring a couple of years ago. Adders like to bask in the sun out here on the hills, but they also hide in the undergrowth. So be careful where you walk and try to stay on the beaten tracks rather than go wading through the grass or the heather. I thought I'd nearly trodden on one once, and it gave me one of the frights of my life because they're poisonous and can give you a nasty bite, but luckily it turned out to be this skin."

"Eeh, Miss, do we have to go? I'm scared!" said one of the lasses from Wylam.

"Howay man, woman, divvent be a scaredy cat. Come with us, and we'll kill them with this stick," came the reply from one of the Willington Quay lads.

"Now you don't have to go that far, mind you. You have to respect the animals, not attack them. There aren't very many anyway. I've been here loads of times and I've hardly ever seen any, and only the one close up. And even that turned out to be this dead skin! What you might see at the most could be some swirly circular tracks in the dust near the rocks, where they've been playing in the sun. Just stick to the paths and you'll be all right. Now split yourselves into archaeology teams of three or four and let's all go and investigate!"

It didn't take long for the kids to be scattered far and wide across the landscape. As you'd expect, it was more to do with high spirits and getting up to mischief than archaeological zeal!

We looked down on the hive of activity going on below us which was setting the merlin and sparrowhawks soaring and the red grouse flapping into the air. The flocks of horned Scottish blackface sheep and the Cheviot sheep, the ones with white faces, must have wondered what was going on.

"We're a couple of bear-washers on the quiet, Linn, you and me!"

"What on earth do you mean, Dodd?"

"Oh, it's one of my favourites. The Germans have a saying, 'Wash the bear, but don't get the fur wet.' I picked it up when I was there. What I mean is, look at all these willing slaves we've got doing our work for us, searching for new clues, while we can stay up here and enjoy the view. 'I love work. I can sit and watch it for hours.' Who was it who said that? That's more or less the equivalent to the bear-washer story."

At the end of the hour and a half the teachers gave them to come up with some discoveries, it took a lot longer to round the classes back up again than it had to split them.

"Goodness me, by the state of your trousers and hands, I can see you must have been really busy getting down to some serious archaeology. Your mams are going to be really annoyed with your teachers and me for letting you get into such a clarty mess," said Linn, tutting and shaking her head.

"So... who thinks they know what the cup and rings are? Let's hear some ideas. Come on, then, shout them out!"

"We think they're like rings on a cooker where they used to cook their food. They put oil in the cup and set fire to it."

"Well, that's a very inventive idea. Well done. Any more?"

"They're religious marks, before people invented the cross."

"Or like signposts or maps showing you where the next hill-forts are, and the rings are how many walls they have around them."

"Ah, but remember I told you the marks were probably done a long time before the hill-forts were built."

"Well maybe they're just signposts and the circles show where the hills are."

"Or could they be stars and planets going round in orbits, Miss?"

"Well, that's certainly another idea, though remember it was only a few hundred years ago that modern people began to believe again that the earth wasn't flat and that the planets went around the sun. In fact, your idea is a very good one because it illustrates an important point to remember in archaeology: you have to try to think like the people in the past thought, with the knowledge that we suppose they had at the time. So we can't ascribe modern ideas and knowledge to ancient people – I mean we can't at all assume that they thought the same way as we do now - otherwise our guesses will be wrong. Of course we can't know for sure what they thought. Maybe they did believe that the earth was round and rotated around the sun, and then their ideas were lost in history and the same ideas were only re-discovered thousands of years later. After all, the ancient Greeks and Romans knew the earth was a globe. The Greeks worked that out thanks to geometry – so don't think geometry's a waste of time! And then it was the Church that insisted the earth was flat. Until hundreds of years later Galileo proved again that it wasn't. But there's me going on too long again, when I should be listening to you! So any more ideas, please?"

"How about they could have been used to grind grain to make flour? They could have had another round grinding-stone to fit into the cup and rings and grind around on top of the rings and they could have poured the grain into the cup and the flour would have come out of the channel. What do you think, Miss? Me and Bobby thought of that and we tried it with a stone and some seeds we found and it sort of worked."

"That's really interesting, Bobby and…?"

"Joe, Miss."

"Yes, Joe and Bobby, excellent work! Especially for the way you went on to the next step and you actually did an experiment to test out your idea. Just like real scientific or industrial archaeologists. Well done! You'll have to show all of us your experiment on the way back down to the coach."

"Please Miss, can we show you ours too? We got our penknife and we made our own cup in a rock. It only took us about half an hour to make a hole the same size as the ones the Stone Age men made!"

"I'm not so sure that's what I was wanting you to do, girls. You're not supposed to go round making fake cup-marks. Though I suppose there's no law against it. At least you've taught us that it didn't take such a long time for Stone Age men to make these markings. Though of course they didn't have penknives! Anyway, I hope you won't do any more in future! Now where's Joe and Bobby?"

"Here, Miss!"

"We will certainly come and see your experiment!"

"Oh thanks, Miss! Hey Bobby, we've got to find our grinding-stone again! Can we go and get it ready, Miss?"

"Just let me say one last thing then we'll all follow you to your stone. What I'd like to say is that you've all obviously got really brilliant theories about the cup and ring markings. I think you've given us some new ideas that even the experts haven't thought of. And I hope you've made some good drawings and descriptions of the interesting archaeological finds that you've discovered too. I'll read through all of them over the next few days, and I'll let your teachers know who the winners are. Make sure you put your names on your papers, so we know who did what! Now, let's all follow Bobby and Joe! Lead us to your archaeological experiment!"

CHAPTER SIX – THE PROFESSOR

"Linn, why so early?" I asked, as I held the phone in one hand and rubbed the sleep from my eyes with the other.

"We are going to meet a professor friend of mine at the University."

"Which University? Is he young and handsome and does he drive a Porsche? If the answer to all three is yes, I don't want to know."

"Not the former Poly - what's it called now? Oh, that's it, Northumbria. The other one. The former King's College. And he's old and alcoholic and drives an Austin A40."

"Sounds like the kind of professor whose friendship I should encourage you to foster."

"But he is handsome in an old and alcoholic kind of way, mind! You should've seen him when he was younger."

"Oh, I'll allow him that. But hang on, that kind of person doesn't start work before about eleven. At the earliest."

"Did I not mention that we were going for a jog on Long Sands first, like? We've got to start our joint training some time, haven't we?"

This was something worth getting out of bed for. Bracing air, crashing waves, glistening calves - what more could a man desire?

The drive down the Coast Road was a dream on this bright and clear morning. We sped along in the eastbound carriageway past the old baccy factory, with its smell which always reminded me of bread-and-butter pudding when I was little. The cleaning lady at Hanover Lofts told me that quite a few of the Toon players live in the converted apartments there now. It's close to the Benton training ground after all. At the same time, we saw the westbound commuters grind to yet another halt in their cages as they began to stack up on the approach to the city. I couldn't help noticing an Austin A40 among their number.

"I got that song you were talking about, 'Racing in the Streets'. It's really good. Have a listen," said Linn as she slotted a CD into the player, "In fact I've heard lots of his songs. And I was very impressed by his pianist."

I gulped, "You what? How would you know that?"

"Well, I've seen him on a DVD," Linn replied, a little puzzled.

"Well, I don't know what kind of DVD you've been watching, but I've never seen him with his kecks off, so I'll have to take your word for it."

"Pianist, I said. Pianist! You need the cotton wool blown out of your ears, Dodd, and that's a fact! The sea breeze'll do you good in more ways than one."

"You had me going for a minute there, Linn! It's the noise. I must get the exhaust fixed on this car."

The first sight of the sea as you hit the final segment of Coast Road after the last roundabout before the Park Hotel is always a joy. But under a cloudless sky it is without parallel, at least in the known world as I know it. Parking next to St George's Church on the Cullercoats seafront, we jogged down to the sands and soon our bodies were thanking us for the superhuman effort we had made to get out of our beds and down here to one of nature's most invigorating interfaces. The white horses out there in the breeze were never going to win this race as we sprinted towards the old swimming-pool in front of the Grand Hotel. This was wonderful training for the Great North Run, still quite a few months off. A couple of lengths of Long Sands and we were set up for the day, and we would pass any exam the professor could set us, I felt.

***

"Where's the parking?"

"Eh?"

"Sorry, Linn, it's me being away on the continent for so long. The French and Belgians call a car park a *parking* and I got so used to hearing it that I say it myself. I know it makes me sound weird."

"Certainly does!"

"The funny thing is, when you ask them what the proper French word is, they can't easily think of one, because the real ones sound so long and awkward compared to their garbled English words. Like if they have to choose between saying *le parking* or *l'emplacement de stationnement*, you can guess which they choose. They also talk about *le camping* and *le footing* meaning jogging – they like putting *'ing'* on the end of an English word and using it as a noun instead of a verb. Then you've got awful words like *wellness*, meaning wellbeing or getting fit. Though they've apparently borrowed that directly from New Age Yanks, without passing by the OED. There are lots of others that sound silly in English but fine in French despite the best efforts of the *Académie Française*, which helplessly tries to protect the French language from the Anglo-Saxon invasion."

"Well it serves them right. They invaded us in 1066 and brought plenty of French words with them!"

"Yes. *Touché*, I suppose they'd have to say, ha ha. They certainly have a lot to answer for - those forty 'immortals', the members of the *Académie* - arresting the natural development of their language for more than three hundred and seventy years, and enforcing academic and archaic Latin-inspired spellings which didn't even exist until they invented them. They're not even proper immortals - though they've managed to conspire to consign their poor language to a living death."

"How would you know, Dodd? If they're immortals or not?"

"Well, who is?"

At eleven-thirty we entered the Antiquities Museum. Outside, the University precincts had been a hive of activity, with students milling all around the quadrant and a steady stream going in both directions through the arches under which the exam results would be posted within a few short weeks. This was, after all, getting close to the start of the examination season. The foyer of the museum, just around the corner from the arches, could not have provided a greater contrast. It was a haven of peace and timeless tranquillity.

"Linn, how wonderful it is to be seeing you again."

The 'wonderful' was long and drawn out, in a central-European accent. Maybe Austrian, maybe further east.

"Professor, how well you look." Linn was so chirpy, her still-flushed cheeks bearing witness to the run on the beach.

In truth he looked awful, and Linn's earlier description had been very accurate.

"And this must be Dodd that you were telling me about on the phone. Dodd, welcome to you. You are most welcome indeed."

"Thank you, Professor, I am honoured to meet you at last."

Hadn't the heart to tell him the first time I'd heard of him was about three hours ago. But Linn had filled me in and my interest in what he had to say was real enough. Apparently he was one of the UK's leading experts in Roman history, and his specialist interest was the reign of the Emperor Hadrian. The Romans themselves had taken an interest in the local history even back then, and in particular in the local gods. When excavating the Governor's residence in South Shields, the Professor had come across a number of rock carvings which just could not have been Roman but which pretty much fitted in with the same pattern as those which were still to be seen at Lordenshaw.

"But come on through," the Professor was saying.

"A cup of tea, perhaps? At this time you probably are wanting a cup of tea?"

"Oh that's very kind of you, Professor. Mind these are special cups, though but," I replied.

"Take a sip and try it first, my boy, then I will tell you…"

"Mmm, very good," said Linn.

"How does it feel to know that you are drinking from the funerary urns of two Bronze Age persons?"

"Uhhh?" we both spluttered.

"Hah! My little joke! Do not fret yourselves. These are exact replicas made from the same kind of clay, taken from the riverbed in Upper Redesdale," smiled the Professor.

"Oh, very... very good, Professor. Well, whatever they are, real or not, I'm somehow not thirsty any more, thank you very much!"

"As you wish! I try it on all my visitors. It is most amusing, you agree? So... now... let's go straight through and I shall show you our little stony friends, yes?"

We followed the Professor through the museum itself, with its wonderful model of Hadrian's Wall as centrepiece, flanked by Roman gravestones and memorials erected by Legion commanders thanking their Governor for his generosity in laying on this or that facility. Nineteen hundred years old history staring us in the face. You could almost hear the metal-on-stone sounds of their hob-nail boots as they marched along the Stanegate. And the bark of the centurions' Latin, only half understood by the Arab, Syrian, Thracian or German squaddies in the wet wilds of Northumberland, hundreds or even thousands of Roman miles from home.

At the far end of the museum the Professor stopped in front of a door in the corner. After some Laurel-and-Hardy fumbling with a bunch of keys, he found the right one and opened the door. He led us into what appeared to be a dusty storeroom. After he had finally found the switch, the light revealed a kind of morgue of antiquities. Gravestones, milestones, plain old stone stones, some of them draped over to no apparent end. All just old stones to the untrained eye. And no doubt over the centuries farmers and others had had no qualms whatsoever in using similar old stones for whatever purposes they saw fit.

"This is where we keep our cup and ring marked stones. Come look, Linn, and you too Dodd. See."

"When we're trying to work out the meaning or the use of the cup and ring markings, we have to know something about the kind of world their creators were living in. Otherwise we can come up with crazy guesses which have no bearing on reality."

Linn glanced across at me, as if to check whether I recalled that she had said the very same thing to the children up on Lordenshaw. I smiled and nodded in what I hoped she would take to mean my acknowledgment. Maybe she'd learnt it from the Professor. Or maybe he'd been on one of her guided tours and heard it from her?

"So what are your thoughts on the markings, Professor?" I asked.

"I shall tell you. We now are thinking that the first markings date from the New Stone Age, which means four, five, maybe even six thousand years ago. This was around about the time that visitors or traders or settlers from abroad were coming into Britain and showing the locals how to be growing crops and becoming farmers. The newcomers also brought in new plants such as wheat and barley, and then later came new animals like pigs and sheep that none of you British had seen before. The beginning of farming would have changed the landscape, with clearings being cut through parts of the forest to make space for crops and flocks. I believe that you could not imagine the hills of Northumberland without sheep now, but back then they were, like you say, a new-fangled import."

The Professor obviously liked to display his mastery of our language and idioms. I was intrigued by the fact that although his English was well-nigh perfect he had kept such a rich accent. A bit like Henry Kissinger, I thought.

"And rabbits," he continued, "well, they never saw them at all, but not because they were invisible like Harvey."

"Like Harvey?"

"Yes, the most famous film with James Stewart. You must know it. The big white invisible rabbit. Very popular in Slovakia. No, there were no rabbits because they didn't arrive until millennia later, when the Romans marched in. The locals would probably have thought they were from outer space and started worshipping them – the rabbits, not the Romans, that is. Which reminds me, there's an international conference on prehistoric rock art in Bratislava a few days from now. It would be well worth going for both of you. Now where was I? Oh yes, farming."

"You might think that farming would have been a big step forward, and that they'd have been jumping for joy. Like rabbits! Or the other rabbits with long legs... let me see... hares, yes, hares. Asking themselves why they didn't think about it before in the last two and a half million years. Think again: back then it would have been really hard work being a farmer when you just had very simple tools to work with. Having to dig the ground, plant the seeds, do the weeding, cut the harvest, grind the grain, and so on. Compared to all that work, the hunter-gatherer life might still have been a most attractive prospect. If you were a gatherer, you would just pick and munch on whatever berries or nuts you could find in the bushes, or wild grass or weed crops you could rip out of the ground whenever the pangs of hunger struck. And if you liked meat, as I am sure most of your British ancestors did, hunting wild boar and cattle and deer, or fishing in the rivers was most certainly not such a bad life either."

"As long as there was plenty to go round. And some of my most esteemed colleagues say this may be the key: both ways of life would have gone along in parallel for a long time in the three thousands BC, with the change to farming accepted, possibly reluctantly, as the only way to feed the growing population. So they would have gradually changed from nomads following wild herds throughout the seasons into farmers settling in one spot, growing food and rearing cattle, goats, sheep and pigs."

"Even when they began keeping animals, it took them a long time to go from only using them for their meat and skins and bones to also keeping them for their milk, which they might well have kept in pottery containers. Though people had known for quite a while how to make it from clay, pottery came into wider use around about the time they stopped moving with the herds. This was because it was too fragile, yes, too breakable to carry around with them from place to place. And using the wool to spin and weave cloth came a lot later still."

"We are possessing some most wonderful examples of rock carvings here. Take a look. You see the characteristic deep central cup, the circular rings around it? And then many also have a radial groove running through the rings into the cup. Or does the groove go out from the cup and through the rings? Nobody knows which way round they were supposed to be in our ancestors minds when they made them."

"As I said before, we think these markings may have originated any time between four and six thousand years ago. But here is an interesting fact: very similar circular markings, even down to them also featuring a radial groove, have been found from a much later period. These are in eighth to third century BC graves in a quite different part of the world, Greece and its colonies. Can this be a coincidence or could the Greeks have seen the

Stone Age cup and ring markings on rocks at one of the rare sites where they appear in Europe?"

"Not so long ago, I was invited to give an address at the Museum of Archaeology of Catalunya at the site of the ancient Greek colony city of Empuries. The emporium. This lies in a beautiful location between the little old village of Sant Marti de Empuries and the larger town of Escala on the coast of Catalunya, an hour's drive north of Barcelona... I am thinking I am sounding a bit like a holiday brochure... Excuse me, but I did so much enjoy my visit! The sun, the anchovies, the Faustino wine, the dinner at *El Bulli* in the evening. A most wonderful experience. Ah, yes! Completed by the discovery of one particular exhibit - a carving on a gravestone of a Corinthian warrior's helmet and his *soliferreum*, his spear made all of iron, rolled-up to render it unusable and looking very much like a cup and ring marked stone. So this stone had a figurative meaning, but is it not remarkable that it is so similar to these cup and ring markings? This particular example was dated to the sixth century BC when it was found at Empuries. But, as usual, I am straying far from my subject. Do excuse me."

"The Bronze Age reached Britain some time around 2,000 BC. You can guess from the name that the big change was that people learnt how to make bronze tools, weapons, armour and ornaments by melting copper and tin together. Making weapons shows that it was not really a peaceful time, though it must have varied from one place to another, and of course weapons were also needed to hunt animals, not just for fighting. At the same time, agriculture was developing, with more forests being cleared to provide open land for growing cereals and grazing animals. It was also about 2,000 BC that the first woven cloth appeared in Britain."

"Through the hundreds of years during the last part of the Bronze Age from around 1,000 BC and into the Iron Age, which began some time shortly before 600 BC - many centuries after the Greek Iron Age began, by the way - your ancestors were building more and more complex designs of walls and ditches and stronger fortifications at hill-forts like Lordenshaw. No one can really be sure whether the fortifications were to defend against enemies, or a show of status, or to provide shelter for the people and their animals. And we're not sure if they were lived in all year round, or only seasonally. Whatever the reason, their construction would have been a huge communal effort, requiring most intense planning and leadership."

"The Iron Age saw the introduction of a combination of new skills to extract iron from the natural ore, to build kilns capable of reaching the very high temperatures needed to melt iron, and the blacksmith's art to work the iron into useful tools. These skills possibly were brought in by Celtic people, who seem to have gradually arrived in Britain over a period of a few hundred years at about this time. For your region it must have been very important, because iron ore could be found naturally here, whereas copper and tin and bronze had to come from outside the area."

"So the people who first started making the cup and ring markings on the rocks at Lordenshaw were there long before their descendants who built the Iron Age hill-fort. Unfortunately, there is no trace remaining to show us how and where they lived. All we can see are their rock carvings."

"What's this big one here, Professor - the one covered in a white shroud," I asked as I lifted the sheet. This one particular stone was a bit different from the others. Or at least the inscriptions were.

The Professor pursed his lips, almost imperceptibly.

"Ah! That one. We have no appropriate place for it in the museum."

"Is there something special about it?"

"This is not two thousand years old," the professor was saying, "it is at least four or five thousand years old, I believe. Though I have colleagues, they say no, it is Roman. But I say nonsense!"

This he shouted.

"My contention is," he went on – did he think he was addressing some conference now, I wondered – "that Governor Gaius Julius Verus – he was the one who ordered that the Antonine Wall in Scotland be abandoned and Hadrian's Wall reoccupied, you know – he had this stone excavated in Northumberland and brought to Arbeia, South Shields. But look again at the face. It is not contemporary with the cup and ring markings. In fact I believe that it represents the cult of Mithras and it was added by the Romans."

"I've heard of Mithras. There's a Mithraic temple on the Wall, isn't there?" I asked.

"Quite right, Dodd. It's at Carrawburgh, on the military road - General Wade's military road. The road whose foundations were filched from the very handy supply of stones stacked up neatly in the guise of Hadrian's Wall, thus destroying long stretches of it."

"Well, they needed a road. The Romans couldn't expect us to leave their wall just as it was forever. After all, they rode roughshod over a lot of people and their possessions themselves, didn't they? Like this stone itself - it's a perfect example of the way they stole things and destroyed them," said Linn, getting all het up too, a bit uncharacteristically I thought.

"Now, now, Linn!" the Professor interrupted, "The temple was found by a farmer in a marshy bog in the middle of one of his fields one hot summer when there was a severe drought which uncovered part of the temple. Now the interesting thing about the Mithras cult is that its origins lie in Persian and Indic cultures and it spread westward across the whole Roman empire through Arabia, Africa, Thracia, Dacia, Hungary, Germany and eventually to the northernmost frontier of Britain. As you know, the Romans were quite open to adopting local gods and beliefs from other cultures into their own."

"Mithras was a brave, honourable and true man who trapped a mighty bull and sacrificed it in a dark cave so that its life-giving blood could benefit all. Mithras was thought to have been born or reborn from a rock – from what is called the *petra genetrix*. It is said that followers of the Mithraic cult believed that the cave represented the cosmos seen from within, while the rock represented the cosmos seen from outside. Hence the possible interest that the Romans might have had in this and other such rocks. You can appreciate how rocks fascinated and held an attraction for all kinds of people from different times and cultures."

"Roman soldiers who were stationed in the far east of the empire might well have learnt of Mithras from natives of the eastern lands who were themselves conscripted into the Roman army. No doubt Mithras's qualities of valour and honour were valued by the soldiers, and for this reason a significant number of them became followers of Mithras, though it seems to have remained a secret and mysterious cult. They hid their temples in caves or cellars to resemble Mithras's dark cave where he had slain the bull."

"I imagine the Roman governor wanted the rock taken back home to his villa outside Ostia as a souvenir. Who knows, he might have been a secret believer himself. But I am supposing it slipped his mind. I am thinking that he probably had other, more pressing matters to attend to."

The rock's dimensions were impressive. It must surely have weighed a ton, if not a ton and a half. How on earth did they move it back then?

"The Romans had no business doing that," grimaced Linn.

I broke the awkward silence.

"Thank you very much, Professor. You've given us a lot of your valuable time. That was wonderful. A personal tutorial. We're most grateful. Aren't we, Linn?"

"Oh yes, most assuredly. What you said about the conference in Bratislava sounded very interesting."

"I have the honour to be on the International Organising Committee, though I won't be going myself. But if you'd like to go, I think I can arrange to have the fees waived for you."

"That would be most generous, Professor. I think I'd like to take you up on that. And you, Linn?"

"Let me just look in my diary. As long as I am back for the erm... twenty-seventh, yes, that would be fine. Yes, I would love to go."

"So. I will arrange it. And when you're back, you must be coming and telling me all about it."

"Of course, Professor. It will be an honour. Until then, goodbye and thank you most sincerely."

We strolled back to the parking, sorry, I mean car park. I couldn't believe my luck. It sounded like the Professor had set me up with the chance of an away weekend, or even a week, if that's how long the conference was going to be, with this angel of the north. And she sounded quite happy at the prospect.

"Mind, he certainly goes on a bit, doesn't he? It was like a lecture. The words just kept pouring out. But he is very nice. And very helpful. Now we need to get onto the Internet and find out how to get to Bratislava, wherever that may be."

All that Linn replied was, "The capital of Slovakia. I have a friend there. But they still shouldn't have done that."

"You're not still on about the Romans, are you, Linn?"

"Yes? And so should you be!"

Hang on... What did she say? Friend? Who was this friend, then? I could see my daydreams staying dreams.

CHAPTER SEVEN - BRATISLAVA ROCK ART CONFERENCE

"They'll be ordering you to switch that off in a moment. And if you don't they'll stop the sketch and call in the police. They will."

"I just want to tell me friend Pat everything's okay. Bit of a worrier is Pat."

I still hadn't got much information out of Linn about Pat. Except that they had been really good friends and had known each other for ages and we were going to be staying in Pat's flat. She obviously was taking great pleasure in knowing that I knew that she knew that I was not enjoying not knowing whether this Pat was her girlfriend or her boyfriend. She was making the most of it at every opportunity.

"There, I've sent a text."

"Now switch it off then, and give Pat a call when we get to Vienna."

Just in time really, because no sooner had she switched her mobile off than the announcement came telling everybody to turn off any electronic gadgetry they might have, but especially mobiles, as they could interfere with the plane's navigation systems. And we didn't want that. We were already taxiing towards our take-off position, and the roar and slight sway of the aircraft were reminding everybody that it was too late for the nervous to change their minds. This is the point where I always have second thoughts. Normally my routine sees me through. Keeping my nose stuck firmly into the newspaper. Reading intently. That's it. Don't think about anything except what the paper is telling you. Before you know it you are in the air, up a height, above the clouds, and somehow that is the bit I find easier to handle. I can even begin to enjoy the experience, at least a little bit. Normally.

But today is different. Because it is Linn's very first flight. Ever. Yes ever. And suddenly she has become very nervous. I think the sight of the flight attendants pacing up and down and doing their final checks hasn't helped. It kind of makes everything seem so suddenly very now and very final. It's now or never.

"Cabin crew be seated for take-off, please." Here we go.

I know her fingernails are going to leave a lasting impression in my arm. That's it. The engine roar rises to a new peak and as we hurtle along the runway we are literally pressed back into our seats by the force of the thrust. A great feeling of helplessness. I realise she is truly terrified. Her eyes screwed tight shut and I feel so responsible. I look out and it is still the countryside around Newcastle Airport that is flying past. But a second later we can feel actual lift-off and we are the ones who are flying. Up we soar and the rooftops are soon tiny. We circle Newcastle, and I can easily pick out the New Saint James' Park Stadium, the eighty-thousand-seater citadel majestically dominating and proudly guarding its city. Paid for with the money they made from two consecutive Champions League titles. (Some say that the rarefied air up here can make you hallucinate.) Mind, the view from Level Nine is pretty much like you get from this aeroplane. It's good that most people are now starting to drop the 'New', like they did with 'New Pence'. Wasn't it a great relief to see sanity prevail over the 'save our dogshit' brigade in the public inquiry into the re-siting to Leazes Park? Now we've got the finest stadium in the UK, regular home to internationals, and FA Cup and European Finals.

The pilot in turn picks out the river and we quickly pass Howdon gas-yard and then Tynemouth and sail out over the sea. There's the ferry headed out for Amsterdam. It is six in the evening, so the time would be about right.

But now there is a thick blanket of cloud. And really we could be anywhere on the planet. Anywhere in the fairyland of cloud-castles and faces and figures. All smiling in the brilliant sunshine that they are denying to those in the real world below.

Her eyes are open again now and she turns her head in disbelief as she looks down upon the clouds basking in the sun. She turns her head back to me with the look of a little girl lost in wonderment. You've looked at clouds from both sides now, pet, as someone once sang.

"I thought you'd be well used to this. How d'you get to your advanced years without ever flying before?"

My reward was a nasty nip. And a question: "When do they bring the drinks round? I could murder a G and T. And you're right – but the only flying I ever do is in my dreams!"

A couple of hours and a couple of drinks later and we began our descent into Vienna-Schwechat Airport. The flight magazine had told me that it was not far from the Slovak border and that we would actually be flying into Slovak airspace as we made our final approach. They're even marketing Bratislava as the Twin City of Vienna. Two capitals which are closer to each other than any other pair of capitals in Europe, if you see what I mean. I had told the flying virgin sitting next to me all about the 'bump' phenomenon. And that if we were lucky we wouldn't feel anything at all. As a result she was clutching my arm as if hanging on for dear life.

The bump came, as it always does, and mind it was a beauty.

"Never again," I heard Linn say as the flight attendant was welcoming us to Vienna, where the local time was a quarter to nine in the evening and the outside temperature a very pleasant nineteen degrees.

***

"To visit a conference on prehistoric rock art in Bratislava," was my smug answer to the passport control officer's "Vot is the purpose of your fisit to Austria?" His even smarter reply was "Hef a nice time in Pressburg."

"What was he talking about? Where's Pressburg?" Linn was asking as we followed the signs to the metro through an airport so antiseptically clean it could easily be used as a giant operating theatre in the event of some major disaster.

"Oh he was just being funny, that's all," I replied.

"Pressburg is the German name for Bratislava. Be careful not to use it when we get there tomorrow. The Slovaks can be a wee bit touchy about that, I've read." I'd been brushing up on the plane with my copy of Fill Roads' excellent guidebook, 'Bratislava – ye canna whack it'.

The state-of-the-art-plus metro put on an impressive show as it whisked us silently into the city centre. We had jumped on just as it was about to leave and hadn't had the time to buy tickets at the machine. But the ticket inspector was well used to that and had no objection to selling them to us on the train. Although I hadn't handled euros for a while, I wasn't fooled by the two Bulgarian one-lev pieces she tried to palm off on me in my change. She was so sorry, but they were really so similar. Pull the other one, pet. Nice try.

It was getting on for half past ten by the time we alighted at *Karlsplatz* underground station. When we emerged into the street above, the nightlife of Vienna was just getting into full swing. A neon swirl of revellers bent on having a good night out. After checking in at the Hotel Sacher – you have to splash out sometimes, don't you – we decided a little walk around would be just right after being cooped up in the silver bird, and anyway we might bump into Harry Lime.

Even though we didn't see Harry himself, we were definitely in his booth in the Prater Park's giant Ferris wheel the next morning. We knew this because carved with a penknife into one of the wooden benches was 'Harry Lime was here'.

"I hope that doesn't mean you are the third man," said Linn.

"Tell me who the other two were and I'll kill them both."

A sharp dig in the ribs was my reward. The view of Vienna was breathtaking but the Danube, disappointingly, was a sick shade of brown rather than blue as it flowed sluggishly towards the Slovak border on its long journey to the Black Sea, by which time it would be black and blue all over.

On the skyline we could see the Vienna TV Tower, where one time I'd seen people doing bungee-jumping off the top. You could just go up, pay through the nose, and they'd strap a length of elastic around your ankles and push you off. I heard a rumour that if you couldn't afford the high price, they had a special offer of a twice-as-long bungee elastic at half the price. Not for me, I'm afraid.

On the tram-ride back to the station we passed a massive overground bunker which was all of fifty metres tall and looked as though its walls could be a couple of metres thick. The Nazis' twentieth century answer to the hill-fort defences.

"Maybe that was Hitler's Vienna town bunker," I ventured. Only to be corrected by an old Austrian busybody who told us that it was a public air-raid shelter. All the big cities of the Reich had had them. It looked very odd, a concrete monolith in a small park surrounded on all sides by old apartment blocks.

Our train left the *Südbahnhof* at 11.33. It was Slovak rolling-stock and the contrast with the Austrian trams and metro trains we had been on was massive. The rickety compartment we were in with its curved wooden panels, faded red flock seat coverings and old windy handles to open the windows reminded me of a cross between the interior of an old pub on Shields Road and the old electric trains that used to run to the coast on the North Tyneside loop. And the pace was slightly more sedate as we trundled out through the Viennese suburbs and through some very lush green countryside completely bereft of the Sound of Music mountain backdrop we had been half-expecting.

We could hear the opening and shutting of compartment doors further along the corridor and coming our way as the Austrian and Slovak border-guards did their rounds. Slovakia is now part of the European Union of course, but not yet part of the Schengen zone, so everyone's passport is inspected. Twice over.

"Ah, so you are British." She actually got it right and didn't say English. "You are most welcome to the Slovak Republic." And with a quaint "Please" she handed us back our passports. Her Slav accent was so much easier on the ears than the harsh guttural tones of her Austrian colleagues. And in her blonde and tight-fitting, long-legged lady passport officer sort of way she was dead sexy to boot.

Looking out of the window, we could also tell the difference in the houses. The Austrian ones had been so prim and proper and completely over the top in the floral balconies department. Here in Slovakia the plaster was flaking off the walls of most of them, and you could tell lots of the roofs actually needed replacing rather urgently. The roads were dusty and potholed, and there were weeds growing out of the tramlines. You could just imagine Michael Caine or Richard Burton stepping down from one of the old trams in a long shot of a dusty street, only to be arrested by the secret police in long grey greatcoats. No wonder the customs lady had said we were welcome to Slovakia, I thought, a wee bit unkindly. The tatty houses made the nice smart ones stand out all the more. Most of these featured impressive fences with matching curtains and closed-circuit TV cameras. Obviously the abodes of those who had managed the transition from real existing socialism to brutal capitalism rather more successfully.

After the post-imperial and still highly pretentious splendour of *Wien Südbahnhof*, the *Hlavnà stanica* station was a reminder of Bratislava's rather more modest place in history, and its homely sort of atmosphere was not a little reminiscent of Tynemouth station in the old days before the Metro arrived. And like I said, the train itself would not have looked out of place rolling into Tynemouth either. But at least the station had money machines, and soon we were proudly in possession of several thousand crowns. We felt like royalty. *Koruny* turned out to have about the same value as old Belgian francs at about sixty to the pound, so it was fairly easy for me to get the hang of them. But the smallest of our notes was still far too big for the short taxi-ride up the winding cobbled streets following the tramlines that pointed the way up to the castle, the *Hrad*, overlooking the Danube. We were a bit surprised when he drove us the wrong way up a one-way street, but we later learned that this was perfectly acceptable, and even encouraged. Under the one-way sign there was a notice advising the driver to 'go ahead, but at your own peril', and also at the peril of the poor unfortunates driving down in the proper direction. Generously tipped, the taxi driver went on his way a happy man.

Here we were just a couple of hundred yards from the castle that had put the 'burg' in Pressburg and literally in the shadow of the conference centre adjacent to the parliament building. Linn double-checked the address, *1892, Palisady*. There were a couple of bars just down the street. Maybe I'd get a chance to pop in some time. This was the right place, the flat of her friend Pat, the cultural *attaché* or, I hoped, *attachée* at the British embassy. It wasn't until Pat opened the door that my worst fears were realised. It was *attaché* without the extra 'e'. But Pat turned out to be a really canny Geordie lad.

After greetings and chitchat, Linn and I had an afternoon nap while Pat sorted some paperwork out at the office. The Ambassador was on a routine debriefing trip to London and the mice were doing what mice do when the cat's away. When he got back – I mean Pat, not the Ambassador - Linn was finishing her shower and ten minutes later we were strolling on the riverbank side of the castle looking out across the here somewhat bluer Danube and over towards the Austrian border some ten kilometres away. Pat knew the distance pretty exactly and also the time it took to jog there and back, which he frequently did.

"Do you take your passport with you in case you fancy popping into Austria?" Linn asked.

"I've got a sort of diplomatic ID with me all the time, and once I had to show it. And the first few times they took photos of me. Just as if it were still the Cold War. But now all the guards know me and are very respectful. Did you know that the river used to be the border? Up to the end of the Third Reich, that is. There is even a famous picture of Hitler standing in a meadow just over there on the other side. With the castle in the background for full effect. As if to say 'We'll be marching into your country next'. Not that they needed to, mind. It was pretty much a puppet régime. The Slovak and German footie teams even played against each other during the war. Can you believe it?"

"Who won?"

Well, I was curious.

"The Slovaks, of course. It was here in Bratislava. The crowd went wild, apparently. It was the only opportunity people had to show openly nationalistic emotions. But either way it was a propaganda coup for the Germans. Showed that life was going on normally and good friends could have a game of footie. And hey look, you won. Isn't that sporting of us? But of course the German players – half of whom had to be Austrian – got a massive bollocking and were probably threatened with a posting to the Eastern Front if they didn't buck their ideas up. I've often thought that would be a useful sanction for Newcastle United players as well."

Our conversation came to an abrupt halt when we looked over the low wall of the steep riverbank and there below was a young Slovak lass spread-eagled on a thigh-high broad parapet with her legs dangling over the edge towards her boyfriend, who was leaning over her. They only had eyes and hands for each other and were keen to let nature take its course notwithstanding the odd passer-by.

"They're, em, very care-free, the young ones, aren't they?" was Linn's question.

"People reckon it's still part of the rebound after Communism. For decades, nobody was allowed to do anything without the Party's approval, so now everybody does what the hell they like. It's the same with the drink, as you'll no doubt see later on in the Old Quarter. Anyway, after the war, Czechoslovakia claimed those meadows on the other side of the Danube, and proceeded to build those horrible endless blocks of flats. That's the Petrzalka district. They're all built out of pre-fabricated concrete panels and so the nickname for that part of town is *Panelaky*. Rhymes with 'gallopin pie-yackie'. It makes you think of plasticky panels, and that's what the whole place looks like. Of course, up to the end of the First War, this was all part of the Austro-Hungarian Empire. The street signs in the Old Quarter are in Slovak, German and Hungarian."

This we were able to see for ourselves only a quarter of an hour later, by which time we had wound our way down the narrow, sometimes hairpin lane of the riverbank. The Old Quarter, the *staré mesto*, was absolutely buzzing. On a par in all departments with the Quayside of a Friday evening. Though Linn reckoned the scantily-clad girls here would be deemed to be slightly over-dressed in the Bigg Market.

"This is Hviezdoslavovo Námestie, one of the major squares," announced Pat, "it's named after the national poet, the bard of Bratislava, Pavol Orszagh Hviezdoslav."

"It's easy for you to say that, Patoslav Geordskie! And what's that swanky old building over there, then?"

"That's the Carlton Hotel. We sometimes hold receptions there, and very nice it is too!"

After our little tour of Bratislava's Quayside, which included a small but beautiful baroque opera house, Pat took us to a wonderful old half-timbered tavern called, bizarrely enough, the 'First Slovak Pub' where the terrace seats gave us a grandstand view of the comings- and goings-on. The pub had fourteen different rooms decked out with scenes from different periods of Slovak history, including what looked a bit like Vandals and Huns and Goths and knights and crusaders and pagan gods.

We ordered some hamburgers off the Slovak-English menu. But when they arrived they turned out to be bread and cheese. Obviously they lose something in the translation, namely the beef. If only Ronald Reagan had been here, he could have asked for us, "Where's the beef?" But he's never there when you need him, is he? So we asked the waitress for a recommendation of what we should have to complement the cheeseburgers, and we plumped for the wonderfully named *Winky*

Palacinky, which turned out to be a kind of stuffed pancake. Between sips of *Zlaty Bazant* beer and a Slovak clona-cola called *Kofola* for Linn, Pat asked, "So what exactly is your conference about?"

"Well, experts from all around Europe will be giving papers on rock art. You've got the paintings and sketches drawn on the walls of caves, like in France, and then you've got the carvings on rocks, some figurative and some purely symbolic like in Northumberland. There are a few places around Europe with rock art rather similar to ours in Galicia, Sweden, Norway, the Swiss Alps, Scotland and Ireland."

"Sounds fascinating. Will the papers be in English, Slovak, German?"

"I think I read there would be six languages altogether, but simultaneous interpreting is being laid on."

"Well that could be fun."

"How do you mean?"

"Don't get me wrong. These professional conference interpreters are really good. If the organisers are paying for proper interpreters, they'll be good, don't worry. But sometimes really funny things can happen."

"Like what?" Linn was fascinated.

"Well, for instance, I went on mission a few years back to Bruges... Sorry, in the real world that's a business trip, isn't it? But in the Mickey Mouse world of British diplomatic circles and watercress sandwiches, it's called a mission!

Christ, it's as if we are trying to convert the buggers. Which I suppose is what I'm actually supposed to be doing as cultural attaché. But all I managed to convert was Slovak crowns into Belgian francs at the time. Anyway, it was a conference on the 'Cultural impact of third-world nations on the world stage'. Load of bollocks, more like! There were participants from just about everywhere and there was simultaneous interpreting into and out of all the languages concerned. It was at the Erasmus Conference Centre, as I recall. Funny they called it that, because he only stayed there for a few months, did old Erasmus. Nice plush place for fat cats in the centre of town. But full of mosquitoes, mind you. Too many stagnant canals."

"There was some German Professor Doctor Doctor somebody or other giving this *spiel* about the meaning of the European enlightenment, or endarkenment, when the English interpreter says 'The Professor is now telling a joke. Now German jokes are almost always impossible to translate, as they often as not depend on a play on words. So I am not even going to try, as I have slipped up too often in the past. Instead, here's one of mine which I prepared earlier.' Well even that got a laugh, at least among the Brits of the Valerie Singleton and John Noakes generation."

"And then he told this joke about interpreting for a French politician from Normandy. Apparently he was making a speech saying that, faced with some difficult political decision, what was needed was a good measure of wisdom, something for which the Normans themselves think they are famous. They call it *'la sagesse normande'*. Seizing his chance, our interpreter announced to the audience listening in on their headphones that 'To solve this problem, we need some help from Norman Wisdom.' Well at that all the Brits in the room were creasing themselves. Only trouble was, nobody else was laughing. In fact everybody had a dead serious look on their face. We found out later that while our man was still in full swing with his joke the Professor had finished his and had gone on to say something about a dear colleague who was renowned for his sense of humour but who tragically couldn't be with us as he had died of a heart attack the previous weekend. It just goes to show that initiative can be a dangerous thing."

Linn and I exchanged glances that said, "Are we allowed to laugh at that?"

We weren't sure, but we did anyway.

***

After the warnings at Newcastle University about the probably primitive facilities at the Bratislava conference centre, we were more than impressed. The glass-panelled main conference room afforded a view of the fairy-tale castle on the one side, and a Danube panorama stretching into Austria on the other. The air conditioning was in fully operating order and the giant LCD screens dotted around the room gave each of the five hundred participants perfect insights into the speakers' subject matter.

The Conference Chairman, Professor Dubnica, speaks.

"Good morning and welcome to the Seventeenth International Conference on Rock Art."

Absolute silence.

"I'd just like to begin by telling you something."

He paused for a few moments, just long enough to make everyone wonder.

"Something I learnt a couple of weeks ago when I gave a talk over in Kinsale in County Cork, Ireland. Some of you may know that there are important examples of rock art in the Cork and Kerry mountains – that's why I was over there. Now it's a funny thing, but whenever you begin a talk by saying 'Good morning', you don't really expect that many people are going to answer, do you? Well, this time everyone in the whole room wished me a very cheery 'good morning' in return. I was quite taken aback. I thanked them most kindly for their very warm welcome and began my talk. Afterwards, I asked Professor Gallagher, who is also with us here today, why this was."

"And being a good Irish Catholic, he had the explanation. This only happens with an Irish audience. And why? It's because just about everyone attends mass, you might even say religiously. The parish priest will always begin the service with the same 'Good morning', and the whole congregation's instinctive response is to reply in unison with a loud and clear 'Good morning, Father.' Putting myself in the priest's place, if this conference were taking place in County Cork, I should now say, 'May God be with you' and you could reply, 'And also with you.' Or, as they say in Latin: 'Dominic have the biscuits come?' To which the response is: 'Yes, and the spirits too!" All of this pre-amble to prepare you for next year's conference, which, as it has just been decided by the Steering Committee, will be held in County Cork. But today we have the pleasure to be here in Bratislava in these wonderful facilities provided for us through the generosity of the Government of Slovakia."

And then the conference got under way, with plenary debates, academic lectures, workshops, poster sessions, and exhibitions. Quite an interesting phenomenon to a conference neophyte like Linn. The academic rivalries, the barely suppressed jealousies, the jockeying for position. And amongst it all the passion and the enthusiasm and the sheer interest of some of the talks.

A young PhD researcher gave the most interesting lecture as far as we were concerned.

"My name is Max Thracoslav and I'm a visiting researcher from Bulgaria, deeing a PhD in the Archaeology Department at the University here in Bratislava. I'd like to give yiz a short presentation based on me researches into cup and ring markings found around certain specific regions of Europe. I've called me paper 'A prolegomenon to the spread of cup and ring markings from region to region.' First slide please. Cheers! Here you see the central cup with its circular rings and a radial cut running through the rings into the cup. You often find cup marks without any rings at all, sometimes on the same rocks which also have the more complex cup and ring markings, as shown on the right of the slide. The majority of the markings are found on rocks out in the open air, but they've also been found inside rock shelters and in burial sites and cairns. Second slide please. Ta. Here you have an interior view of a burial cairn. It is thought by some researchers, including myself, that there were beliefs amongst prehistoric man that the rocks were the gateway to the world of the gods and that they passed through them to reach their dwelling-places below ground."

"Other more recent cultures also held special beliefs about stones. For instance, we know from the Viking sagas that in Iceland, where there are many boulders strewn across the landscape, they believed that the rocks actually were gods or trolls who came to life at night and slept during the day. Another example is the Roman belief in birth from a stone. These are very similar kinds of belief which are actually documented in writing."

"People wonder whether previously-marked rocks from earlier generations were put into the burial sites, or whether they were newly made for that express purpose. Current thinking is that the people of the late Neolithic Age were the first to produce the cup and ring markings. They would have had a definite use or meaning at the time. But maybe then things and people moved on and perhaps the practice fell into disuse, though of course the stones remained. Then perhaps in the Bronze and Iron Ages, people may have re-discovered the stones and given their own meaning to them, perhaps the same as the original meaning, perhaps very different. In the same way as the swastika was adopted by successive cultures. It originated more than four thousand years ago somewhere in Asia, contemporary to our cup and ring markings. The word actually comes from Sanskrit and means 'wellbeing'. So it came from neolithic times, then it was adopted by many different cultures, for instance by Hindu, Jewish and Buddhist religions, by knights of the crusades, and even by the Boy Scouts in their early days, before its meaning was irredeemably changed by the Nazis."

"So it may have been with the cup and rings. Later generations may have re-used the old stones or possibly created new ones of their own. One of the big problems is that there's nee equivalent to carbon dating for stone, so it's difficult to tell the age of the markings except by indirect deduction. This also means that you can't know whether the cups without rings were made long before the more complex markings, or whether they were all done aroond the same time and by the same people. Or whether people came along later to add rings around cups made by earlier generations. Or to add carvings of animals or humans, as you can see in the different examples on slide three please, from Sweden, slide four please, from Galicia, and slide five from the Swiss Alps. It all adds to the mystery."

The close-ups of the Galician stones were breathtaking for us Northumbrians, as they were remarkably similar to ours, except that they included figurative art too. The question is whether the cups and rings were made at the same time as the figures, or before.

"So you have seen that we find similar markings in various places but they're never quite the same. In the New Grange burial mound in Ireland, and especially on the famous gateway stone, they are spirals rather than rings. Slide six please. In the Hordaland area near Bergen in Norway and in the Bohuslän region on the Norwegian/Swedish border, the cup and rings are often incorporated as a motif in the body or shield part of stick figures carrying spears. As an aside, Hordaland is well worth a visit, not only for the rock art but also for the magnificent scenery in which it is set. If you ever go, take the train ride up from Bergen to Myrdal and then switch to the Flåm railway and you'll see just what I mean. Slide seven please. Cheers. Cup and rings in the Alps on the Italian-Swiss border are also found as motifs within or alongside representations of human or animal figures."

"Whereas the Northumbrian ones, as on slide eight please, are never found in conjunction with figurative art. There also other variations in Muros and Baiona, near Vigo in the Galician border region between Spain and Portugal, where animal carvings are often found alongside the cup and ring markings, as you see here on slide nine. The Galician examples along with the Scottish rock art, slide ten please, found around Argyll on the west coast, Dumfries and Galloway in the south-west, and Perthshire in central Scotland probably have the closest similarities with the Northumbrian ones."

"It's funny how many of these places happen to be in modern border regions, though of course the borders did not exist at the time of the carvings. And on that thought, I would like to conclude my talk. Thank you very much for your attention. Cheeors. Oh, and Ahoy!"

Even before Max had stepped down from the podium, Linn was on her feet.

"Let's go and have a chat with him, Dodd. I think I've seen or heard him before. There's something about him."

"It's funny, that, because I had the same kind of feeling, Linn. Déjà vu. I'm sure I've come across him too."

"Hmm, well, we can ask him. He said some very intriguing things about the meaning of rocks to different people and cultures and about how the cup and ring art spread to different places. Let's catch up with him before he disappears off somewhere!"

"That was a very interesting talk, Max. My name's Linn Rorting and this is Dodd Law – we live in the North-East of England and we're really interested in the cup and ring markings in

Northumbria, but you've shown us a lot of new things this afternoon."

"Ta very much. I'm glad you enjoyed it."

"Nice to meet you, Max. By the way, what's a prolegomenon?" I asked.

"Oh, it's just a word that people in our kind of field use to make things sound good, like. Ye knaa, a buzzword. Like some academics used to use 'paradigm' and 'paradigm shift' back in the seventies and eighties, and then all kinds of numpties in the nineties and noughties started to use it. It won't be long and you'll be having prolegomenons, or should I say prolegomena, on the telly."

"So what's it mean?"

"Well, it's not as good as it sounds. That's why it's useful, I suppose. It means an 'introduction', that's all!"

"That's it?"

"Aye, that's it!"

"Bit of a disappointment, then."

"Aye. But it soonds good!"

"Did you take all those photos yourself?"

"Aye, I did, thanks. I've spent the last few years on this project, going to all the different sites. Northumberland is one of the best places for rock art. You're lucky to live there."

"We definitely are! We noticed you've got a Geordie accent too. It's just that both of us kind of thought we've seen you before somewhere. Did you spend a lot of time there?"

"Actually, no. Just a couple of weeks. Ye knaa how Aa got it? It's because Jamie who teaches English doon in the British Council here in Bratislava is a Geordie, and we didn't knaa the difference, man. He says I'm a natural at picking up the accent. Mind, he's a champion teacher, the best they've got."

"Whey man, that's great. A bit o' propa culture in the British Cooncil. Just what they need."

"Can I just ask you another question?" interjected Linn, "What was that 'Ahoy' for at the end of your talk?"

"Ye haven't heard them saying it here yet? It means hello in Slovakian. And it also means goodbye!"

"Well, that's a bit strange of them to say 'Ahoy!' in a land-locked state, isn't it? You know, like ship ahoy," remarked Linn.

And then I thought, "Aye, and it's a good job the Beatles weren't Slovaks, otherwise it would have spoilt a perfectly good song. You know: 'You say Ahoy, but I say Ahoy.' It doesn't have the same ring to it somehow!"

"That's good, mind. I'll have to tell Jamie that."

"We're interested in going to see some of the other sites. Where would you recommend?" asked Linn, getting us back on track.

"Well, I can give yiz the exact locations of some geet good rock panels in Norway, Sweden, Ireland, and Galicia. If I were you, I'd start with one of those. Whichever suits your time and pocket.

There's also a really good Internet discussion forum where you can log on to get advice. There's a poster with all the details about the website on that wall over there."

"That would be a great help! Do you fancy some bait and a pint?"

"Whye aye, man. Sounds a good idea. Let me just get me notes together. Have you tried the *Prazdroj* in the toon, near the Opera? It's actually a Czech-style pub. You know *Pilsner Urquell*? Well *Prazdroj* is the Slovak equivalent to *Urquell*, meaning the original source, the water spring. Greeit place. Jamie'll probably be in later on too. Howay, I'll show you the way."

We had a great night with Max, Jamie and Pat, who took us around all the sights and sounds of Bratislava. We made a special point of congratulating Jamie on his mission to get the unsuspecting nation of Slovakia taaking Geordie instead of English. He was meeyekin' a fine job of it. Along the way, we got some good tips from Max on the best rock-carvings sites to visit. And he taught us something else about conferences:

"Now here's a question for you all," said Max.

"If you have to choose between going to a conference or a workshop or a symposium, you know which one you should choose? Any ideas? No? Well I know! Where I come from in Bulgaria used to be part of Thrace, next door to ancient Greece, and the answer is 'the symposium'. And you know why? Because it's ancient Greek, meaning 'drinking with companions'."

Which is exactly how we spent our last evening in Bratislava.

LORDENSHAW

Chapter Eight – New Moon on Lordenshaw

"Are you allowed to have these cup and ring-marked stones, Linn?"

"Aye, Dodd. I am! They're mine! These are what are called 'portables'. Stones which have been removed from their place of origin. Often they were so small that a person could carry them on their own, though some had to be dragged or moved by horse and cart. You can find such panels all over. There's a famous example in St John Lee's Church, just north of Hexham, and another on the site of the Corstopitum Roman fort at Corbridge. These ones that I have here have been in my family for so long, no one remembers where they came from."

She ran her fingertips over the smooth contours as she spoke. She crossed the room and leaned over a stone table.

"This one's my favourite," she said, with the faintest hint of a blush appearing on her cheeks. It

113

was a single ring with a radial gulley leading into the deep cup.

"You see this runnel here? Would you like to run your finger slowly along it and tell me what you think?"

She took my hand and placed my fingers onto the smooth surface of the stone as the beginnings of a smile lifted her upper lip, exposing a glimpse of her tongue between the even rows of teeth.

"How does it feel?"

"It's so smooth, it almost feels like flesh."

"It gives me the same feeling."

"Now gently approach the cup hole."

She guided my hand and time slowed and stretched out.

I guided her hand.

"And how does this feel?"

"Like rock."

She paused a moment.

"I think we should go to Lordenshaw… now."

"Now? At this moment?"

"Yes. We must go tonight."

"But it's night time and a new moon."

"Exactly."

"But it'll be pitch black."

"And so?"

"You really mean it?"

"Yes… bring some woolly blankets, and I'll bring the rugskin, and my pipes, and an oil-torch."

We parked in the dark and deserted car park, lit our oil-torch, and stumbled up the hill to the fort, where Linn led the way to a large, smooth outlying rock. It was the one where I'd given my smallpipe an airing. The light from the flickering torch picked out its cup and ring markings, and Linn selected a particularly deep cup and wedged the torch into it, as if she'd done it before. We spread the rugskin over the rock panel and climbed on top to take in the view, wrapping the blankets around us. For a moment I had visions of adders slithering in to join us, but tried to suppress the thought. The night was still and the sky was overcast so we could see no stars. The lights of Rothbury and the isolated farms and hamlets dotted the countryside in the valley below. The air was cold, but we were warm under the blankets. And soon warmer still.

***

I touched her shoulder and asked why she was crying. Someone crying makes me uneasy and I don't know what to do for the best. So I babbled something inane.

"Is it the bracken? It's growing taller by the day. My eyes itch and stream from it. Look!"

"No. It's not that. Not at all."

For about half a minute she said nothing, just a few more sobs. She sighed and said, "I knew we would end up... making love. I knew all along, right from when I first saw you. Through the school railings. There was something familiar about you, like I'd known you before. It was as if I had seen… done… been there before. I have dreamed it a thousand times. Oh, long before we met. I have these dreams, well it's the same dream, really. Sort of… it varies, but it's the same dream. Same people, same faces, same things…"

"People?" I interrupted.

"Yes, people. Same everything in fact. Even the same trees."

"Oh come on, you can't know it's the same trees."

She turned her face towards me abruptly and shot daggers from her eyes.

"Yes I can. I'm telling you, they're even the same bloody trees."

Stroking her hair, I apologised. "Go on, tell me about the dreams. The dream."

"I've never told anyone before. It's been too important. It happens so often. Sometimes every night. Sometimes just once a week."

"Go on."

Nothing. Minutes passed. More sobbing. Her breathing became more regular again and she began talking, her head still turned away from me so that I had to listen that much more intently. I knew instinctively I was not to interrupt.

"It's as if I'm flying." A pause.

"No, this is stupid. You'll only start laughing at me. You saw how I was on the plane."

I say nothing. A minute or so of complete silence except for our breathing. The torchlight flickers in the darkness.

"It's as if I'm flying. Or hovering. Or floating. That's it. Floating. Around here, over Rothbury and the Coquet and the Simonsides. Over all the hills and fields and farms. Then I soar, yes soar. The cloud is sucked from under me and I feel the rush of air and then it's up and up, and then free fall. Never-ending free fall. It slows right down somehow and there I sink through swirling mists that make me feel like I am being absorbed by time itself. The swirling icy-hot mists of time, you might say." She giggles, then sniffs.

"Two words go through my mind. I can't make them go away. Longing and belonging. Longing is belonging, I know it is. I become a part of it as we begin then to plunge to what feels like a couple of hundred feet above the treetops. It's the same place. It's our place but all the buildings have gone. It's so rugged, the craggy rockfaces and hills. And the greenery is so grey like in late autumn. There are a few of us tending cows. It's time to take them back to some kind of enclosure marked out by a crude wall made of rocks. Some kinds of shelters made from the boughs of trees. Fires smoking and the smell of wood burning. And the sounds of the talk. Strange sounds. Almost a wail, a shriek, a bark as a mother calls her child. But it is their language. Our language. It must be. I understand. Dressed in the crudest of clothes made of rough cloth and animal skins, they all are. And I understand what they are saying, I tell you.

How the hell can I? I don't know, I just don't know. I feel the sounds within me too. And the smell of the autumn air. Richer than now, I can't explain why. The wet earth, I feel and smell. I breathe it in greedily as if feeding on it, depending on it for my vital nourishment. I soar again and it feels like my soul has been ripped from the body. Yes, ripped."

Some more sobs, then silence.

"It's the mists again. It's time itself, and I have to part it with my hands, rive it asunder. I see more people, new people, coming. I feel them ... murdering the new generations we left behind. And I mean feel. I can feel the blows, the stab of the sword. It penetrates, enters me."

Another silence. Again I say nothing. I cannot possibly interrupt.

"Some mingle with the new. Sometimes it's inter-marriage. But generally it's rape. Either way, new life emerges. Mostly, though, ours stay among themselves. There's a... a straight line. Yes, a straight line. And I follow it, in my dream. It's my... guiding thread. My path. The sounds change. Not just the sounds but the structures, the melody. Till it's completely different. One moment I'm in the air and next I am in the ground. Part of the ground, tasting and breathing the earth. I feel the rock, run my finger along the patterns. Become part of the rock. Must be dead, I suppose... No, this is stupid. You must think I'm stupid."

"No. Not at all," I tell her. "And this you keep dreaming over and over?"

"Much more. Much more. It seems to go on forever. The place changes as new people come and then more new people. And always the sounds change. The clothing changes. Their language changes. And I understand them. It's because it's always the same people, our people. Those in charge, at the top, they are different. But the villagers on the hill, it's always the same stock. Always has been. I recognise the faces, the same features. It all sounds very crazy, doesn't it?"

"No." I don't know what to think.

"And always near the end, just before I wake up, the pipes. Simple pipes, not like the pipes we play now. Gentle notes brought along on a gentle breeze. But they get brisker as the lament reaches some kind of climax. That's what I have been trying to create. Why I want to call my lament 'Longing is belonging'. There's much more to the dream but there's plenty of time for that. I don't want to talk about it any more this evening at any rate."

And in so saying, Linn took up her pipes and played her lament around and around, very quietly and very slowly.

"It's very beautiful. And so are you."

We fell quiet as we contemplated the view, and then quite suddenly the lights below all went out. Another power cut, I supposed. Just a few campfires or torches flickering away like ours.

"This is what it must have looked like thousands of years ago."

There was no reply from Linn. She'd fallen fast asleep in my arms. It looked like we were here for the night. And why not? It wasn't as if I had anything better to do. In fact I couldn't think of anywhere I'd rather be.

Over the last few weeks, through every moment in each other's company, we'd grown used to being with each other, to each other's temperaments, without revealing too much of ourselves to each other. I'd always found this difficult before, and it had been no different this time. Tonight there had been a change - Linn had needed to open herself up to me. Her thoughts and dreams. I felt somehow obliged to do the same. But it was as if she already knew everything, or everything she needed to know. As if she had recognised something in me or knew what even I might not realise about myself.

I was soon asleep, but it wasn't a restful night. I kept hearing sounds. Adders! And badgers and foxes and maybe even feral goats, and rabbits of course, and then the sheep. Rustling the grass, snuffling about, grunts, squeaks, and groans. Be quiet, Linn! No, I think it was the animals. But Linn tossed and turned, talking first to herself and then in a one-sided conversation or more like an argument at one point.

I even dreamt myself seeing her having the argument with a wiry, shadowy figure then turning away in a fury. Then chasing around with a dog like the girl of a few weeks ago. Then catching a vole or some such animal, which she cooked for our breakfast, using her burning torch. Tasted not too bad, actually. I woke with a start just as I got to the line, "Eeh, that roast vole was champion, Linn. Time for me te gan an' chisel oot a new sign on a rock, pet. Work to be done! I'll be back hyem later."

Dawn was breaking and Linn was already up and folding away the blankets. I was all tangled up in the fur skin. Must have looked like a caveman. Only one set of lights was on, across the valley in the hills behind Rothbury. Very appropriately, it was at Cragside, the home of Lord Armstrong, the Newcastle engineer, and I remembered having read that his house had been the first in the world to be lit by hydroelectricity, and so the only one around with its own power. An instant later, I looked again and all the lights were on.

***

"Big power cut again last night," I remarked to the petrol-station attendant, as I looked at the poster advertising the upcoming Rothbury Traditional Music Festival.

"Whatya on aboot, man? Wiv had nee pooer cuts up here fo' years."

CHAPTER NINE – THE ROTHBURY FESTIVAL

"This Traditional Music Festival's been great hasn't it, Linn? Years ago, I was at the Northumberland Gatherings in Morpeth and Alnwick, but it's the first time I've come here to the Rothbury Festival. And the weather's been perfect all day. Ideal for sitting out here on the village green watching this impromptu session. It's lucky they hold it in the summer."

We were right in the middle of the village, enjoying the interplay between the pipes, fiddles and accordions.

"I'm glad we saw the advert. Mind, it's just as well we checked up on the timings because Saturday's definitely the better day to come, as it looks like most things wind up at lunchtime on Sunday."

"I've really enjoyed it too," replied Linn. "All that talent, and all the work and practice people have put in to get themselves to the different levels they've reached. It's nice there's a place for everyone – you don't have to be a prodigy to get up on the stage and play. You just do your best. Something on top of your everyday life at work, or out of work, or at school, or in retirement. It's wonderful really, don't you think? Especially the pipes competitions. I really was nervous going up there, but once I got going, I managed to find my way through well enough not to embarrass myself. I suppose that's what adrenalin's for."

"I thought you did really well, Linn. I was proud of you, getting up there and playing like that."

"And I was proud of you, too, Dodd – stopping in your tracks and beginning again after you made a total cock-up of the first couple of bars! It kind of broke the ice for everyone to be able to have a good laugh. The way you made a joke of it, and didn't get nervous. By the end I think you got the biggest cheer of all, even if you did come in second last."

"Beaten by a nine year old! Mind, she was pretty good. Next year my aim will be to beat her. I've already got the measure of her seven year old brother!"

"Aye, it really was good. I knew I wasn't there to win any prizes, but it was just good for the experience. Some of those young children are amazing players. And the workshop on the history of the pipes was brilliant, it really was. I learnt a lot."

"Me too. I thought the pipes would have been a lot older than just three hundred years or so. I imagined the locals frightening the Roman invaders with them nearly two thousand years ago."

"The pipes supergroup in the Jubilee Hall down at the bottom of the village was fantastic too: the William Lamshaws, father and son, and all the rest: John Dunn, John Peacock, Robert and James Reid, the Clough family, and Billy Pigg. A dream ensemble. I don't think we'll hear their like again. And then it was just over the road and into the Queen's Head for the carvery and another music session. What more could we have asked for?"

"You're right, Linn, I'm absolutely stuffed. Aye, it was hard to choose between there and the Newcastle Arms and the Turk's Head."

"Which explains why we ended up going to all three, I suppose!"

"I suppose… Hey look, they've got a record stall over there. Had ya hosses man, woman, don't go charging off. Let's see what there is."

"I'll be back in a minute, man. I'll just go and buy one of those delicious-looking carrot cakes we saw before and also some cheese with wild cranberry from the stalls in the farmers' market."

"More food! Well, I'll be here browsing through the CD collection."

It wasn't long before Linn was back, laden down with home-made goodies.

"You're right, Dodd. It's not bad at all, is it? I think it's the same people who run the stall in the

Grainger Market. They must have come up for the weekend to sell some of their folk stuff."

"Linn, I wouldn't mind another pipes CD to remind me of what we've seen today. Tell me if you see any. I've only got Billy Pigg and Kathryn Tickell, and that's all... Hey, look at this, Linn: 'Lordenshaws' by Kathryn Tickell. Well, there's a real coincidence! I've never heard of it. Our hill, and there's music about it! We can listen to it on the way home."

"We should've had it before, we could have asked her if she'd autograph it for us!"

"If she's still somewhere around, maybe we can. Keep your eyes peeled! How much is that, pet?"

"Ten pounds please. You're lucky we've got that. It's not an officially released CD. It's a recording of a piece for smallpipes and ensemble that she wrote and performed a few years ago. But you've missed her! We saw her go a few minutes ago."

"Damn! Maybe next year!"

At this, Linn just laughed and said she could murder a drink. We'd heard there was going to be a folk session at eight in the evening at the Cross Keys at Thropton, only a few miles away. We were staying in a B&B in the village, so it was a good choice.

***

"So how did you first get interested in the pipes?" she asked, gin and tonic in hand, with ice and lemon, please.

"Well I was never very musical for a start."

"Don't be so modest, man. You're doing very canny. For a beginner."

"But I can't stay a beginner for ever, can I?"

"Well here's to beginner's luck."

And on that, our glasses chinked. Her G and T dwarfed by my pint of Eighty Shillings.

"It was in Northumberland Street. Newcastle's Northumberland Street, that is."

"Well I didn't think you meant London, pet."

"Has London got a Northumberland Street?"

"Well if they have, they don't deserve it. Get on with it, man."

"Aye. Well it was in Northumberland Street. Outside Fenwicks, in fact. I'd been to Thorne's to get a couple of books and had called into the City Tavern for a pint, like."

"Goes without saying."

"And just as I was passing Fenwicks I heard this busker playing the smallpipes. And it sounded great, mind. And plenty of other people must have thought so too, because there were a good few coppers in his cap. I just couldn't believe how wonderful it sounded. Out of respect, or so it seemed, the Chronicle-seller opposite wasn't shouting out the way they usually do: 'Ro'uhgurl'!"

"Mind, you don't really need to shout at all on that patch, do you. I mean everybody buys the Ro'uhgurl. Like some kind of duty. And most of them read the back page first, as part of the same duty, I suppose. Anyway, I just stood there listening. Two or three reels and a lament. I wasn't the only one enjoying the concert, of course. Lots of people had just put down their shopping in the middle of Northumberland Street to stop and listen. The only other time I've heard of people stopping and putting down their shopping on Northumberland Street was when they saw on the Ro'uhgurl placards that Andy Cole had been transferred. Sheer disbelief. They reckon some people were clinically in a state of shock."

"Anyway, the strange thing during the last lament was that the busker seemed to be unhappy after a series of what must have been difficult changes because he kind of contorted his face and sort of whined. Or wailed. As if he were in pain, like. And you know it didn't sound to me at all like he'd played a bum note. Maybe he's just a perfectionist. Maybe he'd played a choyte, a bit like a grace note, when he didn't mean to. Whatever. And you know, it sounded a bit like your lament, come to think of it. Anyway, when he'd finished that one and looked like he was having a break there was a great big round of applause. They all put fifty pence and pound coins in his hat. I waited till the last ones had gone on their way and I put a fiver in his hand."

"I think I know who he is. That was certainly very generous of you. To give so much to someone like him."

"Aye. Well I was captivated, like I said. And, anyway, I had an ulterior motive, didn't I? That's what he said as well."

"What – that you had an ulterior motive?"

"Nah, that it was very generous of me."

"Well how about being generous to me now and getting another round of drinks in?"

It was now only ten minutes or so till closing time and the place was nicely full. Not that closing time would make much difference out here. I knew full well that there would be a lock-in. Through the bar I could see that over by the fire in the other room there were the makings of the folk session. We'd been hearing their songs in the background ever since coming into the pub. Now they were getting a bit noisier and I could see by his face that Jimmy the barman was in a good mood and in the market for a late-night session. His cheeks were aglow.

"Pint of eighty bob and a Tin and Jonic, please Jim."

"There you go, Linn. It'll put hairs on your chest."

"You cheeky monkey. So then what?"

"Well you'll just have to shave them off again."

She picked up the Festival programme lying on the empty chair next to hers and made after swatting me like a fly. I thought it best to continue.

"Anyway, he said it was very generous of me. And I said he deserved it. 'After all, it's a hard act to follow,' I said. And he replied 'Aye. Ya reet there. That blind accordion-player was magic, was'n'ee?' I told him I used to stand there on that very spot with me Mam and Dad listening to him for a good hour after we'd done the messages of a Sat'da afternoon. As our conversation progressed, my Geordie got broader and broader. Must have been my childhood memories coming flooding back."

"Then he stopped me in my tracks by saying:

'So maybe I am the accordion player.'

'But you're not blind, and anyway, I thought he was dead,' I replied, quite taken aback.

'Hey man, 'blind' and 'dead' are very relative concepts where Aa hail from – look at these zombies here for a start.'"

"And with an eerie laugh he swept out his right arm to indicate the madding crowd that was Northumberland Street with its own ceaseless background rhythm of clickety-clack high-heel shoes. Then, as if some spell had been suddenly broken, he said, 'Whye, Aa've had a canny day. Aa think Aa might just gan for a pint.' And I asked him if he minded me joining him for a bit crack."

"He told me his favourite watering-hole was the Midland Bar, nestled in one of the railway arches just down from the Central Station. Said he liked the sounds of the trains you could hear from within. And as we set off towards the bottom of Northumberland Street I told him that my name was Dodd, by the way. His was Charles, but his friends just called him Piper for short. Or sometimes the Mad Piper. He was certainly a strange one. And he was quite a strange-looking figure as well. He must have been only about five foot tall, sort of hunched up. Thin as a rake and grey wispy hair with a wispy beard to match. Kind of a Catweazle type, I thought. Couldn't weigh more than about fifty kilos – oops, sorry, I've forgotten what that is in old money. He walked with a slight limp and kind of stooped over to the right because of it, which made his well-worn donkey jacket flap out and the loose change in its right-hand pocket jingle-jangle, in a joyful sort of way, I thought. He had the gait of a happy-go-lucky Geordie lad in his early twenties who has done his week's graft and is about to enjoy his Frida neet in the Toon come what may. Never mind that Charles, the Mad Piper was sixty-five if he was a day. And mind he had a tale to tell once we were finally ensconced in a cosy corner of the Midland Bar, which must be one of Newcastle's quietest pubs that time of a Friday."

"'So is Charles ya forst or ya second name, like?' I ventured as I sat down with our second bottle of Brown Ale. I never drink it normally, it's far too strong. But when we'd got to the pub he had ordered: 'A bottl'i dog please, pet. For this lad'n'aal. Two schooners.' Who was I to argue with that?"

"'It's not me propa name at aal, man. But Aa once met a gadgy who was really called Charlie Piper and Aa thowt it soonded aboot reet for the loonatic kinda life that Aa lead. So efter that, wheniva anybody asked, that's worra towld them. Noot rang wi that, is tha?' 'Norrataal', said I."

"The Midland started filling up with early-Friday-evening drinkers, mainly middle-aged and older office-workers who wouldn't be getting a proper night out and so were making the most of the brief freedom between work and home. The youngsters were already on the homeward-bound buses and Metros for a quick tea, a quick change and a quick bus or Metro ride back into the Toon or doon the coast for the Friday-evening rituals."

"I was determined not to keep up with his consumption so I agreed to a third but said that was definitely my last. But for my three he had a good half dozen, and remember, this was Newcastle Brown Ale. He freely told me about his life, and about the smallpipes. All the technical details about there being very few kinds of pipes in the world with a stopped chanter, and about the keys and the drones, and how they're much easier to maintain than normal bagpipes because they're blown by a bellows instead of your moisture-laden breath. And then, wait for this, he told me he had worked as an interpreter for the United Nations in New York. My jaw dropped, and after a pause to take in such an unlikely piece of information I said 'What, that little village just outside North Shields?' Don't know if he was amused or not. He just ignored me and went on with his tale."

"He had studied Russian and French at university and then done a postgraduate interpreting and translating course in London, the smoke, as he called it. Then he had landed the three-year contract with the UN, alternating between New York and Geneva. 'The Swiss Alps, the bare rock, my kind of place,' he said. And there he took on another few languages - during working hours, he was proud of that. The UN apparently had a very generous language-training budget. 'Languages - I've seen them come and go, Dodd, come and go,' is what he said."

"I reckon it was the effects of the Broon. I wasn't fooled by his apparently simple Geordie manner. Geordie was his native tongue, he said, then came English, then the others. So really he had interpreted from one foreign language into another. Three-way interpretation, he said that was called. At the end of the three years he had been offered a second contract, this time for five years, but he had had enough. All the travelling back here had taken its toll. He had to be back at least once a month, he said. He wanted back to his people, to where he belonged. Well, I had my doubts of course, but the way he told it made it all sound real enough. After ten years on the continent, and two of them in Brussels, my French isn't bad. So I just tried it out on him and asked him my next question in French. So what did he do when he got back to Newcastle?"

"And he didn't even bat an eyelid. He answered in what for me was flawless French and with an accent to match. He even told me he had a French translator's joke: if Londres is French for Greater London, what do you call the City itself? The

French call it the *Londrette*, he said. Then he had got a job as a shipyard labourer at Swans and it had been the happiest time of his life. And you know the strangest thing of all? I saw him with you in my dream when we were up on the hill!"

"Let's go. Now," said Linn in that peremptory tone mastered only by women.

She would clearly brook no gainsaying on my part. I couldn't for the life of me understand the hurry. She looked upset. Had I said something wrong? I had been so absorbed in the telling of my tale that I hadn't noticed her getting her coat on even as she sat and listened. Next door the folk session was in full swing, but she was clearly in no mood for it now.

"Sure, anything you say, pet."

I threw my coat on and followed after her. Jim had to let us out, for the lock-in was also in full swing, and our steps crunched through the gravel towards the car. Thropton's meagre street-lighting was no match for the spectacular stellar show of universal strength above our heads and we both stood in awe, gazing at the eternal majesty of it all. And from the pub we could hear the pipes.

"It's so glorious and timeless, isn't it? And we are part of it. Always have been, always will be," she croaked.

"*Et in saecula saeculorum*," I had to reply, and kissed her tenderly on the cheek, tasting her salty tears as I did so.

CHAPTER TEN – *A STONE DISCOVERED*

"Dodd, you know that school trip you came on?"

"Of course. I really enjoyed it. They certainly came up with some great guesses about the cup and ring markings, didn't they? Cooker-rings - that was a great one! And Joe and Bobby's flour-mill experiment was excellent, and it just about worked!"

"Yes, I made Joe and Bobby the winners of the competition. Anyway, I've been going through some of the kids' fieldwork again. I don't know how I missed it at the time, but look at this rubbing that one team from Saint Aidan's did. In some way it's familiar, but it's not on any of the known rocks on Lordenshaw. I think one group of kids must have stumbled upon something new. I really need to find it."

"Have you checked with the school?"

"Yes. The trouble is, the kids were running a bit wild, and they can't recall where they found it, except to say it was somewhere out on the moor heading towards the Coquet."

"Well let's go at the weekend. Sounds like the weather forecast is good. It'll be a good day out."

And so it proved to be.

***

"Linn! Come and look at this!"

"Where are you? What have you found?"

"I'm over here in the dip, in a sort of hollow cavern in the side of the bank."

"I'm on my way... Dodd, this is it. It's the place those three schoolkids described on their answer sheet. You've found it, you've found it," she cried with glee as she flung her arms around my neck and we toppled over and right into the cavern.

"This could be Northumberland's answer to the Rosetta Stone," I exclaimed, "You know: the clue that solved the mystery of the hieroglyphics when Napoleon's expedition discovered it in Egypt. Look! It's so well preserved, and you've got these other ancient-looking pieces arranged with the rock. What do you think? Doesn't it give us some really good clues? You know, like if some future archaeologists found a fossilised cricket pitch, but no bats and balls and stumps. Just two sets of three holes, twenty-two yards apart, and a pair of pads and a cricket box or jockstrap. They would probably think it was some kind of place of fertility rites. Then like us finding these other items alongside the rock, they find the stumps and bails and bats and balls and a score sheet. It all becomes obvious: it's a kind of game. What we've found surely will give the same kind of clue to experts like the Professor."

But Linn was only interested in the rock itself.

"It's beautiful," Linn exclaimed, and instinctively she ran her finger along the channel leading through the concentric circles. Above the circle was a face.

"This face shouldn't be here. It didn't use to be here."

"What do you mean, Linn?"

"Look here, there's a face."

Then Linn brushed away some more moss and exclaimed, "A bull! It's like the Professor said. This was added by the Romans. It's the Mithras cult again. They shouldn't have done that, they really shouldn't. Defaced! They've defaced the stone."

"It could be... Mind, when you think of it, it hasn't been defaced."

"Yes it has, it's disgusting what they've done!"

"No! What I mean is they've done the opposite. They've put a face on, not taken it off! You see, they haven't de-faced it, they've em... I don't know... 'en-faced' it. That's it. Enfaced! And come to think of it, we can't say it's been desecrated either – what they were actually doing was making it sacred to their Mithras cult."

"No! That's where you really are wrong. This was a sacred stone, and it has been desecrated."

As she talked, Linn was running her fingers along the grooves, almost lovingly. No, not almost. The playful afterglow on her face had disappeared. She had a deadly serious look about her now.

"This is the one. I'm sure of it."

A little, ironic sort of laugh, quickly suppressed.

"God knows I should be, I've seen it a thousand times before."

"But how could you have seen it?"

"I'm telling you I've seen it a thousand times before."

Now she was shouting.

"And they're right. It doesn't belong here. This is the Lordenshaw stone, or at least it's half of it. It belongs back up on Lordenshaw, not down here. And it has got to go back there. Back home. Just who the hell did the Romans think they were? Vandals! They were worse than the Vandals!"

"That's a good one, the Romans being Vandals!"

"Look, you know what I mean."

Linn was getting exasperated with my high spirits.

"No, this is serious. You know our stone, the one we spent the night on?"

"It would be hard to forget!"

"Do you remember I showed you the marks on the side where someone had quarried off half the rock? They call it the plug and feather technique, and it was originated by the Romans but still used to this day. Well, this is the missing piece. I'd always thought that it must have been taken away and smashed into pieces to build a wall. But here it is, fully intact."

"I can picture the scene. Some damn Roman advance raiding-party was up here and they decided they wanted our stone for one of their Mithraic temples. Maybe even back in the times before the Antonine and Hadrian's Walls. Before we even knew who the Romans were. They quarried it off and dragged it downhill in the direction of the river, where they would have had a barge waiting. But it was too heavy, and the land was so boggy that it literally got bogged down. So they dragged it into this rock shelter in the bank here and made a makeshift temple and secret hiding place."

"Hey, Linn, you could be right. It fits together with what the professor said. You remember - the bit about the Mithras followers always building their secret temples in caves? Well, that's exactly where we are now! In a cave."

"I'm sure I'm right! I don't think this was a permanent temple here. It's too far out in the middle of nowhere even for a secret cult. And it's too small for a real temple. I think they followed their belief, like you said, and put the rock in a cave and hid it, meaning to collect it later. Then for some reason they never came back to collect it. And I hope the reason was that some of the locals waylaid them on their way back to the river and finished them off. And Dodd, what clinches it is that these other items that you said might hold the

Rosetta Stone clue to the cup and ring markings are from the Roman period, not the Stone Age."

"How can you be so sure, Linn?"

"Well, it's a bit easy if you think for a minute… Like, they're made out of metal for a start!"

"Durrr… I hadn't thought of that. Oh well, the quest goes on."

"No. For me, this is the end of the quest. The Holy Grail. Thanks so much, Dodd. You're the one person in the world and in all this time who helped me. I'll be forever grateful to you. You don't know what this means to me. You can't imagine how I've longed for this moment."

"You're losing me there, Linn. You're talking more like it's your family history than prehistory. Tell me the rest in the car on the way back, but let's get a record of this now."

"There's not really much more to tell. Like I told you, it's my dream come true."

"Anyway… It's a pity I forgot my camera, but at least we can make a sketch or even take a rubbing. Here - I've got a good-sized roll of paper and a big soft charcoal pencil. Can you have a go at doing that, and I'll take a reading of our location with the GPS wayfinder. It all looks the same out here and we'd never find it again otherwise. It's going to be dark soon anyway. And I mean really dark, because it's only a couple of days until the next new moon. Our anniversary! We can come back tomorrow and take a proper record."

"Aye, we've found it at the perfect time, just a couple of days to go – we'll have a great anniversary to celebrate."

"I thought we did a pretty good job of celebrating the first time, myself!"

"Well this month'll be even better!"

"I can't wait, in that case."

"You and me both. I've been waiting a long, long time."

"It was only a month ago..."

"No, it's been a long time, too long."

"Sometimes, Linn, I don't know what you're on about."

"Don't worry, Dodd. Better very late than never ever. Giz the charcoal, man!"

We headed back home in high spirits. Linn suddenly remembered she had a very early appointment the next morning, so we arranged to meet at lunchtime.

I was so excited with our find that I couldn't get to sleep, so I passed some time on the Internet forum chatting with other rock-art enthusiasts about our various interests.

But Linn didn't turn up at lunchtime. In fact I didn't track her down until the day after, which was pretty annoying as I'd taken the afternoon off work specially to go back to the find.

I must have rung her mobile a hundred times and at last I got through.

"Linn?" Silence.

"Linn?"

"What is it?"

"Where were you all yesterday and all last night? Are you back home now?"

"No. I'm in the park at Eldon Square. In front of the old houses on Blackett Street."

"I've been up all night worrying and you start talking to me about houses! Where were you? I'm coming round right now."

"You sound like my old granny. Don't get yourself in a state, man."

I walked up through the town as fast as I could. I found her in front of the St. George and the Dragon statue, deep in conversation with the piper. Or deep in the middle of an argument, more like, and they didn't sound much bothered about who could hear them.

"I don't trust you, not after this. It must have been you, you liar. No one else knew," Linn was shouting.

"Well, what's there to stop me thinking exactly the same about you? You're the one who knew first. I don't know what enjoyment you're getting out of doing this just to spite me."

"It wasn't me. You're a liar."

"Whatever you say, Erdlinn. But you'd better be there or else. Do you hear me? I'll be watching you. Always."

I cleared my throat.

"Hey, ha'd on! What's this? Two friends having a tiff? Come on now, cool down… Made a good profit this morning, Piper?"

"And what's it got to do with you? No, if you must know, I've had a really bad couple of days, thanks to this one here. Buildin' aal me hopes up only to have them aal knocked doon igyen."

"Mine, you mean, not yours!"

"Well, I don't know what either of you are getting at, but Linn here's got some explaining to do to me too. Things'll perk up for you, Piper, nee worries. C'mon Linn, we need to go. So long then, Piper."

"Aye… well… so long, Dodd. And you, I'll see you as usual," the piper growled menacingly.

"Is there any point any more? I'm giving up," Linn snapped back.

"You can't do that. There's no choice, do you hear?" he insisted.

"I hear you. But I've stopped listening." And with that, Linn turned on her heels and hurried away.

***

I didn't, or couldn't, look up as I stirred the milk into my coffee. Linn was standing in her blue dressing-gown, arms folded, gazing out over the Newcastle skyline. The clouds suggested a sharp change in the weather soon. A few drops hit the window. Then, as if in mockery, some sunrays caught her tousled hair and somehow highlighted the worried frown that defined her tired face. She looked stunning in her distress. Any other circumstances and my thoughts would have focused on desire. She turned slowly towards me and spoke.

"Look, I'm sorry I didn't show up, alright? I hadn't planned to stand you up. It's just that... something cropped up."

"What, and you couldn't even phone to tell me?"

"I'd forgotten to charge the mobile. Look. I said I was sorry. I met up with a friend. A girlfriend, all right? The one I work with on the school trips, Di. She's had a rough time. Husband's left her. She needed to see me. Badly."

"Me too, I needed to see you. Badly."

"We went for a couple of drinks. Then an Italian. That er... Ristorante Roma place... Collingwood Street, you know... been there for ages... Pasquale's Special: crispy chicken in rosemary and garlic. He's a great chef."

"You don't have to account for your whereabouts to me."

And then half an octave higher:

"Don't I? Well it bloody well sounds as if I do. Things are changing, aren't they?"

"It's not me who's changing. And why do you go seeing that damn piper first, before you even think about calling me? What is it between you and him? All this stuff about him wanting to see you, and you threatening to give up the pipes. I know you're not telling me everything."

A degree calmer:

"It's not the pipes, Dodd. You don't trust me and you're getting jealous, that's it, isn't it?"

"No, how could I be jealous of him. Don't be ridiculous. It's just I thought that you'd be wanting to get back to the rock again straight away. It meant so much to you, you said."

"It does. If only you knew how much it does."

"And there's something else. On the way back from the rock... in the car... what you said... in your sleep. I know you were only dreaming, but..."

"What? What did I say? What did I say, for Christ's sake?"

"You said...'If only I could, I'd kill you, you mad bastard. For what you've put me through. You can have it back. I got it for you. Here. Have it. You were always the same. Now give me back what's mine... what you took away.' Or something along those lines. And then you..."

"What?" And then, at the top of her voice: "You've got to tell me."

"Then you... started speaking in a different language. Or different languages. They sounded different. Like maybe... something a bit like Welsh, then something completely weird, more like a wailing sound..."

"Oh God."

"So what was all that about?"

"A bad dream. A nightmare. A long nightmare."

"Anyway, can we at least go to the rock now?"

***

But when we returned to the site, there it was – gone! And the frightening thing was that there was no sign of it ever having been there. No damp, earthy crater from where wriggling worms and beetles would have scuttled away to get back under the warm, dark shelter of another stone. No, just standing wild grass and bracken growing like everywhere else. And not only the stone was gone, but all the paraphernalia which had been with it.

"Look what's happened now, Linn. With your messing about. We had it in our hands and now it's gone. And nobody will believe us. I hope you and your piper friend are going to be happy now."

"Look, Dodd, what's happened is the last thing I wanted. And the same goes for the piper. I thought he had something to do with it, but I don't think he could have after all. That stone wasn't a 'portable'. It must have weighed a couple of tons. No one could have budged it."

"So who would have done this, Linn? Someone who happened to see us? Who can hoard it away so it won't be found for another two thousand years? Or who thought it would look good cemented into their garden with a gnome standing on top of it? Or was it you and the piper? That's what I want to know. All that argument you were having in the square."

"Now it's you being ridiculous. I just said. Aren't you listening? Of course it wasn't us. And besides, just look at where we are. I can't see how anybody could have taken it away anyway. Look, there's no sign of tyre tracks or of dragging it through the grass. So how did they do it? One person by themselves couldn't have taken it."

"Or have we made a mistake? Is this the right place?"

"It looks right to me. Check your GPS reading, Dodd."

"Well, it says it's right – look. Maybe there are collectors out there who are prepared to pay to have something truly unique. But it's a strange kind of pleasure that they must get out of never being able to show it, or even admit to its existence. And having the personal pride of thinking they're the only person in the world to know the meaning of the cup and rings? Even if they've got it all wrong."

"How are we going to get it back?"

"Well, it's not as if we can report it stolen to the police, is it? 'So you're here to report the loss of a stone, madam? From a field. Hmm, I see... And was it yours? No? Hmm... And how does it look, this precious stone of yours?'... I can just imagine it! There's no point in going to the police. In fact I'm not even sure that they've actually done anything wrong. And Linn, we've got nothing to show, no proof, just some charcoal rubbings that we could easily have made ourselves. It's as if it never existed."

"If I don't find it, my life's not going to be worth living."

"Well, I don't know if I'd go that far, but if you'd turned up when you said you would, this wouldn't have happened."

I said all this, but a thought flashed through my brain and grew into a nagging worry. That damn Internet forum. Anyone in the world could have read that stupid posting I'd made. I didn't dare tell Linn.

A stony silence reigned as we drove back to Hanover Street.

CHAPTER ELEVEN – FERRY CROSS THE NORTH SEA

So step back and take stock.

Sometimes you cannot help reflecting on how quickly and completely your life can change. Perhaps already has changed. And sometimes you just cannot believe the change you have undergone, for better or for worse. Only a few months earlier you had been winding things up in Hilversum, winding up ten years away from home. There had been times when you hadn't realised Tyneside would always be home. Times you had sworn you would never ever go back. But home it always would be. You would always be a part of it, and it would always be a part of you.

Here you are, back home after ten years of criss-crossing Europe, of keeping up with the rat-pack in the vanguard of the rat-race, from Germany to Switzerland, to Belgium and finally the Netherlands. But the money had always been there for the making. And that had always been the carrot dangling in front of your nose. Just a few marks, francs and then euros more, never mind the cost. But you have to make the money. You can tell yourself as often as you like you don't need it. But you do. Sooner or later, with luck, with a lot of luck and a lot of hard work, you have reached the critical mass. You're not rich, but you can get by nicely. Hang on to a job to keep it ticking over, and you will be okay. You are on your own again. And having long since overshot the mark, you can stop aiming at youth. At least that pressure has gone. So get your arse back home while you still can. And home you came, didn't you, bonny lad?

And then along came Linn. And with her came rapid and radical and maybe, if you're lucky and get over the last couple of rocky days, lasting change. And a huge improvement in your piping. And you and she had become lovers. And life had been hunky-dory for you until the flare-up over losing the stone.

Tonight would be the first new moon since that momentous night of the black-out up on Lordenshaw. It was about seven in the morning when the phone in my flat rang. I felt to the right of the bed, where Linn should have been. And then to the left, where the phone was. It was Linn, or at least the sound of her voice.

"Dodd. I'm sorry. Come round here, pet, coffee's ready."

"What the...?" I squeezed the words out of my parched lips.

"Linn's place in ten minutes, or there'll be wigs on the green."

Sundry ablutions and a five-minute shower later, we were having coffee and toast under the massive oak timbers left exposed in the ceiling of Linn's penthouse loft. Eschewing breakfast TV, we savoured a spectacular view of the Tyne being lovingly caressed by a well-mannered sun that had just stepped out of its early-morning bath in the North Sea.

"Why the early rise?"

"Let's go and look at one of the other cup and ring sites in Europe," said Linn.

"What, you mean now? Today? Straight away?"

I was a bit taken aback by the sudden impulse on Linn's part.

"Whey aye man! You only live once! Though maybe for more than just one lifetime."

"You mean it, don't you? The trip, I mean."

"I do. I really want to be somewhere else tonight, anywhere but here. I've been doing the same old routine for too long, and now I want to break out. Just this once, to see what happens."

"Well, if it's that important to you, let's do it! So where do we go?"

"We could go to Norway on the ferry from North Shields, couldn't we?"

"Or a cheap flight to Dublin! Or Galicia sounds like it could be a great place to go, though it would be more difficult to get to. I think we'd have to look for a flight to Vigo through Madrid. It could be pricy. Or maybe fly to Porto, then hire a car. And I know how much you love planes..."

"So let's go to Norway! I think the ferries go to Bergen and Kristiansand or maybe Oslo. Then we can work our way around by train. They have some of the most incredible railway journeys over the mountain ranges and through the fjords. Remember what Max the Bulgarian student told us about the Bergen mountain railway?"

"'Pining for the fjords', are you? Like the Norwegian Blue? It's funny isn't it, they banned Monty Python's 'Life of Brian', the Norwegians. Getting their own back, I suppose. Then the Swedes used it as an advert for the film – 'too funny for the Norwegians'."

"Some of them don't like each other very much, that's for sure. Too much history between them. And between us for that matter - remember the sacking of Lindisfarne."

"Actually, I don't! But I suppose you're going to say I should! Anyway, Norway it will be. I'll go and fix up the tickets."

In for a penny, in for a pound, I thought, as I drove towards Percy Main roundabout, headed for the ferry terminal in the hope of getting tickets for that night's crossing. Glancing diagonally across the Tyne Tunnel trading estate to the left, my mind instantly and automatically recalled a whole host of childhood memories. Trekking up to the blackberry hills just this side of the New Coast Road and on to the Middle Engine, or Middle Ingin' as we called it, almost as far as the Old Coast Road. In those days the boat-train, pulled by a steam engine, would bring passengers all the way from London to the Oslo/Bergen Quay. After its last main-line stop at Newcastle, it would come down the North Tyneside Loop through Wallsend and Howdon and as far as Percy Main, where it turned off onto a spur running up by the Coast Road and down to the ferry.

It was always a favourite sight and an exciting occasion for us local kids, the engine hissing and clanking and whistling as it trundled over its iron road. It was uncoupled and run onto a siding, then reversed past the train to be hooked up at the other end to take its coaches all the way down to the ferryboat. The passengers bound for Scandinavia would return our enthusiastic waves as we wondered who on earth could afford such luxury trips across the great waves of the North Sea.

And where was Scandinavia anyway? We knew even from our primary school history lessons that many of the Vikings had come from there. And the travel posters told us there were mountains, fjords and lots of snow, and pretty girls, all of them blonde. Only years later did I fully realise what a massive imprint those Vikings and their other sea-faring rivals had left on the North-East in the shape of our singsong accent and many of the words we use. For a few hundred years their tongue must have become that of Northumbria, gradually adding to, and enriching the old native tongues and the maybe corrupted loanwords from Latin that must have made themselves at home during three and a half centuries of colonisation.

After going four-fifths the way around the roundabout before turning off, I was soon passing through Percy Main village past the football and cricket grounds. On towards Wet n' Wild and past the Royal Quays outlet centre, on the edges of what used to be the mighty Shell Mex refinery complex to the right and the prop yards to the left.

The whole trip down the Coast Road to the ferry terminal is a stretched-out metaphor for the post-industrial North-East. Where there once stood the factories of W.D. & H.O. Wills, Dunlop and George Angus, Monitor Engineers, Fergusons, Shell Mex and so on, you have apartments, out-of-town shopping centres, multi-screen cinemas, DIY and computer warehouses. Just about the only thing that's left is the Formica factory, thanks to our insatiable desire for fitted kitchens.

I sometimes wonder if a thin veneer of Formica is also in some way a metaphor for the glitz and glamour of the Quayside compared to what you find just up either bank in Shieldfield and Gateshead. Along the Coast Road ribbon and along the Quayside, you've got places to spend money, but where have all the higher-quality jobs gone? The dignity of labour and pride in a skilled job well done replaced by dead-end, casual jobs for students and part-timers. The post-industrial society in a nutshell (mex).

Another few hundred yards and I was at the ferry terminal. Just a few double cabins were still available for that night's crossing and the only outside one was Commodore Class. The thought of being cooped up without a porthole was not appealing, so Commodore Class it would have to be, even if it did mean shelling out a couple of hundred pounds. *En suite* facilities and bunk beds. Yes, bunk beds. Bagsy the top bunk, Linn. Or do you think she might feel like sharing?

It was a nice sunny day, so I suggested to Linn that we might bowl down to Tynemouth for a little walk before driving to the terminal, where I had already booked a place in the long-stay parking, I mean car park. The train could take the strain when we got to Norway. And down to Tynemouth we duly bowled, parking up at the Spanish battery to gaze out between the piers. From the bar outwards the sea looked a bit choppy, but the Nissan boat taking another batch of Micras hot off the Washington production line seemed to be having no trouble. A gentleman walking his dog kindly agreed to take a quick photo of Linn and me with the Priory ruins as a glorious backdrop. Then we set off on our little walk along past the Black Middens and back, enjoying the splendid views of the Mouth of the Tyne and the ice creams, ninety-nine sugar cones of course, which we had bought at the Rea's van in the car park. Ha! Got it right that time.

Great memories here in Tynemouth Village. I used to live just around the corner from Front Street for a while. What a street! How many pubs? Countless. The Gib, the Turk's Head, the Salutation Inn, the Royal Sovereign, the Percy Arms, where the Squad left their guitars hanging up by their necks in the chandeliers with the feedback screaming, and the Collingwood, one of Alan Hull's favourite haunts.

"I suppose the Governor, what's his name ... Gaius something or other, he must have sailed in and out of the Tyne a good few times. Their port must have been right over there, just down from their fortifications. They'll have brought in their Mediterranean luxuries by the boatload, no doubt. Little creature comforts to see them through the dark and cold Northumbrian winters."

"Aye, no doubt," Linn replied, "and I've read that they had a lighthouse on this side, probably where old Collingwood stands now. And no doubt there was some great statue, of the Emperor, or of a Roman god, to remind everyone who was in charge here, on the very edge of their Empire. And they'll have shipped out their plunder by the boatload as well. Including plenty of our people as their slaves. Roman bastards. Oh, sorry, there I go again."

"Ah come on man, Linn, it was nearly two thousand years ago. Sometimes you talk about ancient and prehistoric goings-on as if they happened yesterday. Anyway, they weren't really our people. We are such a mixed breed now: from the original settlers who followed the ice sheet as it retreated to the north at the end of the ice age, to the Votadini, the Gododdin, the Bernicians, the Celts, Picts, and Scots, the Angles and Saxons, the Vikings and Normans, you name it. We're a bit like Heinz 57 varieties really."

No reply to this, but her icy look told me in no uncertain terms that I had said exactly the wrong thing. We walked the rest of the way back to the car in silence, both of us gazing out over the river mouth and beyond at every opportunity.

It was getting on for half past four and we were supposed to check in at the terminal by five for our six-thirty sailing. Twenty minutes and a drive through Shields' early-rush-hour traffic later and we were standing in the queue at the check-in desk. Judging by the number of people in the lounge, the boat was going to be quite full. And these were just the foot passengers, of course. Outside there were several long lines of lorries, cars, dormobiles and caravans, most of them Norwegian or Swedish-registered, but a good few Brits too. Inside the terminal, it was clear that most people were in party mood. The bar was open, and the tables were littered with empty and half-empty glasses and bottles.

Not long after we had checked in, an announcement came over the tannoy: "The Percy Main Social Club trip is kindly requested to proceed to passport control. Travellers with the Evening Chronicle Discover Norway Tour please remain in the lounge until further notice."

"Here we go," I said to Linn, who by now was on speaking terms with me again, "Looks like we could be in for a fun night with Percy Main Social Club at sea."

"Hey, don't knock the social clubs, they're a great North-East institution. They reckon that

157

Abba once played at Cramlington High Pit Social Club, you know."

"Are you sure you're not thinking of Shmabba?"

"No, it was Abba. It's true. I'm sure."

"I reckon that could be another Northumbrian legend, mind. And anyway I wasn't knocking them. Put me down for the bingo."

At that, she was at least smiling again, but we were both treading very carefully with each other after the turmoil of the last couple of days.

When we closed our Commodore Class door and shut out the madding crowd rapidly infiltrating the bars, shops and video arcades, I was so glad I had paid the extra few quid. It was quarter to six and we had time for a lie-down before the boat set sail, which it did at about ten to seven. Linn had commandeered the Commodore *en suite* facilities as soon as we'd opened the cabin door, setting out all of her paraphernalia – her woad, she called it - and leaving no space for mine. Then she'd plonked herself onto the bottom bunk, making it pretty clear that the top bunk was for me.

"I'll be taking the top bunk, then," I said.

"Aye. No, I mean aye-aye, me hearty! Good choice!"

Looking through the porthole, I watched the terminal complex gradually slide away into the background and suggested that we go on deck to take leave of the Tyne in a proper and dignified manner, splicing the mainbrace with a pint in my hand and a G and T in hers. It was a bit of a struggle at the bar, and it would have helped speed things up if the Percy Main crowd had all been fluent in Polish, as the stunningly good-looking young barmaid was having some difficulty with their particular brand of English. She probably thought they were Norwegians. But we got onto the deck with our drinks in time to see what used to be known as the Jungle slip by, followed by those new flats stacked up all the way to the top of the bank. There was the Stag Line building, new Dockwray Square, the High Light and the Wooden Dolly up a height, the Low Light and the Fish Quay down below. Then, as we gathered more pace, Knotts Flats, Lord Collingwood and the Priory in all too quick succession.

Now, as we crossed the other bar and immediately felt the difference we moved to the deck at the very stern so we could take in one hundred and eighty degrees' worth of the river. Gazing up towards Newcastle, we could make out a tangle, or was it a gaggle, of cranes pecking at the skyline. A big proud river, the timeless Tyne taking pride of place in every Geordie heart. Through centuries and millennia it had seen peoples come and go. It had given birth to the ships of Empire, of war, and of peace. It had been pounded by the Depression when its children had gone hungry and shoeless to school. And then pounded again by the Luftwaffe when they hit the Spillers warehouse on the Quayside and blew out the windows of my old auntie's shop a mile away on High Bridge. But it carried on sliding by regardless, and there it was, gradually fading from view together with the long Northumbrian coastline, and all we could see was water, water, everywhere.

Over supper, Linn got out her maps and the Norwegian railway timetable. She was clearly getting excited at the prospect of seeing the Scandinavian rock art for herself.

The party was in full swing when we repaired to the bar, and communication with the bar staff was rendered even more difficult by the volume of the band giving a rip-roaring rendition, appropriately enough, of 'Band on the run'. Then the band ceded their place on stage to the troupe of statuesque Bulgarian dancers who've been brightening up many an evening crossing with their spectacularly skimpy costumes and even more spectacular bodies. They invited volunteers up from the audience, and who should jump up on stage but one of their compatriots who just so happened to be well known to us too.

"Is that you, Max? Over here, it's us, Linn and Dodd!"

"Oh... Hello! The lovely Linn! And Dodd! Me mates from Bratislava! What fettle?"

"Oh, fine, thanks. We're on a trip to see some of the Norwegian and Swedish rock art you told us about. We thought we'd have a trip on the mountain railway from Bergen to Oslo and the ride down to Flåm that you told us about too. And what brings you here?"

"Whey, these lasses for a start! They're from the same part of Bulgaria as me, doon on the Greek border. Canny lookers, eh? Mind, not a patch on yee, Linn!"

He was pished. And I didn't much care for all this 'lovely Linn' business. I'd thought he'd been getting on a bit too well with her in Bratislava and here he was, at it again.

"But how come you're on the ferry?"

"Er... I'm taking a van-load of cup and ring marked stones from the Professor's Museum of Antiquities collection... for a temporary exhibition... at the Oslo Viking Ship Museum. It'll be opening in three days time, so if you'll still be in Norway you should gan along and take a look aroond. It should be really good."

"Is the Professor here too?"

"Nah, he couldn't make it, so he asked me if I'd be interested and available to do it. And being a poor student, the money comes in handy too."

"So you've got a van with you?"

"Yeah, it's a big white Transit van hired from Byker. It gans really well, even when it's full of rocks!"

"Do you think you could give us a lift to the train station when we get off tomorrow lunchtime?"

"Well, it'll be a bit of a squash... but yeah... if you want."

"That'd be great, thanks!"

Our chat was brusquely interrupted when Max was dragged off, not unwillingly, to perform some high kicks and splits by the bevy of Bulgarian ballet belles.

A couple of drinks later and we were reaching our limit. Not of drink, but of equilibrium. It was getting to about midnight and the rocking of the ship was becoming ever more violent as we were overtaken by a major storm. We staggered and crawled our way to our cabin and collapsed onto our bunks. Tonight we were going to be rocked to sleep - and more. By the Devil and the deep blue sea. And through our porthole we could see the stars bouncing up and down.

It was the kind of trip where you felt so sick that if someone had said you were going to sink and drown, you would almost have accepted it as a release from the nausea and squalor. Mercifully, we were eventually released into a fitful sleep.

***

As the rising sun peered through the porthole, I fell awake. We were still out at sea. The storm had delayed us by hours. Was it the light of the sun or Linn's talking in her sleep that had put an end to my dreamland version of how this night with her might have been? Either way, there she was talking to herself again in her sleep as I was trying desperately to gain mastery over my baser early-morning animal instincts. Same pattern as the previous few times: first a series of what can only be described as grunting noises. Could that really be actual language, or was she just kind of moaning or, well, grunting in her sleep? Yet it did seem to have such a regular rhythm, cadences even. She seemed to be asking questions and making statements with these grunts. Then it was something that definitely did have a sound that was recognisably that of a real language.

At times it did sound a bit like Welsh. Maybe it was. Perhaps she had learnt Welsh at evening school. Or maybe she had been on holiday to Welsh Wales when she was little. Aberystwyth or somewhere, where she had heard the language spoken and stored it somewhere in the furthest recesses of her brain and was now just playing the recording. I had read about such things happening, about the daughter of a cleaner at Cambridge University whose mother had dragged her along while she cleaned the apartments of some don or other. The don had been in the bathroom shaving and reciting Ancient Greek poetry. The bathroom door had been open and the cleaner's child had heard it. Thirty years later after a road accident, that same cleaner's child was lying in a semi-coma reciting Ancient Greek poetry. Such things had happened before, so maybe Linn too... Now it was a different language, sounding very like Danish or Norwegian. And now it was clearly thickest Northumbrian, but with lots of words, Norse-sounding words, which I didn't understand.

And then it was her present voice:

"Cannit be there this month. Not this month, not after last time... Got to get away. Cannit be there this new moon. No... not getting me... the bastard... enough's enough. He's got to go back... but not me... He's not taking me..."

After the previous occasions I had bought a dictating machine, the kind that journalists use when trying to coax a soundbite out of a politician's mouth. I had to get to the bottom of this, and I knew just the person to help me, an old friend who lectured in linguistics at Durham University. She knew everybody who was anybody in that field. Surely one of them could work this one out.

But who was she talking about now? Who was 'he'? Was it me she was talking about? We had made love on the rock at the last new moon. Was that why she couldn't go back? Had we, or had she, broken some rule? What the hell was going on? Had our love-making destroyed some kind of protection she had had? I am getting drawn into something here, aren't I? Starting to believe in make-believe? But there is another explanation too – she's just got a vivid imagination, and she's dreaming.

There was a sharp ratatatat knock on our Commodore door and it woke Linn. Stretching and smiling in the warmth of the cabin sunshine, she appeared to have forgotten instantly whatever it was she had been dreaming about. I opened the door to the Polish steward, who marched confidently straight into our cabin with the breakfast tray, stealing only the most furtive of glances at Linn as she hurriedly pulled up the woollen blanket to cover her breasts. He wished us a healthy appetite, in Norwegian. Had he also heard her speaking in tongues as he had padded along the corridor towards our cabin? At all events, on any other day the bacon and egg and toast and coffee breakfast served in our cabin would have been a most welcome start to the day, and infinitely preferable to the hall-of-hangovers buffet affair that was surely going on two decks below us. But we just couldn't face it. Our stomachs had been voided of all their contents and the last thing we needed was a greasy breakfast. A cup of tea and a piece of dry toast was quite enough.

The captain's voice blared out over the ship's tannoy, telling everyone who wasn't still beyond caring that we'd been out in the hundred years storm, the one that statisticians say is so bad that it can only happen once in a hundred years. Trust Linn to choose that night. She'd even muttered something between successive retches about the vengeance of the gods having been unleashed upon us. I wouldn't have been surprised.

We watched through our window-size porthole for the first sighting of land, and as morning turned to afternoon, we caught our first glimpse of the zig-zag mountainous Norwegian coastline and the archipelago of rocky little wooded islands. As we steamlessly steamed closer, we could make out amongst the trees the immaculately-kept little wooden houses in various shades of russet, gold and cream, each with their own boat mooring. A paradise for Viking seafarers. This gave way to the steep and craggy banks of the fjord through whose sheltered waters we were now effortlessly gliding towards Bergen. We decided to have a walk on deck, and sitting at the stern we took in the spectacular Scandinavian show which nature was putting on especially for us. The mountain backdrop plumbed the deep blue depths, a Narcissus bidding to redouble his natural beauty in reflected glory.

When we finally docked, hours late, we'd lost all our enthusiasm for the trip, but we could summon up even less for staying on the ship and facing the wrath of the gods on the way back too. So we sought out Max and clambered into the cab alongside him. In a few minutes, we were at the great, grey stone block of a railway station on the edge of Bergen.

"Can you run in with the two big bags and get the tickets please, Dodd, while Max and I sort out the details about the... exhibition. Here's the code number. You just key it into the automatic ticket dispenser and the pre-paid tickets will pop out. The train's due in five minutes. I'll meet you on the platform. Oh, and just leave me my overnight bag - you can't carry them all."

But the train came and went and no sign of Linn. I abandoned the bags on the platform and ran outside in time to see Max's van driving off in the distance. I raced back into the station and looked up and down the platform, but couldn't find Linn anywhere. So where was she?

Then a message pinged into my mobile: 'Dodd, you and your stupid Internet forum. You lost me my stone. You can find your own way home. I'm off to Oslo with Max.'

The bastard. He must have seen my stupid message on the rock-art forum and told Linn. And now he's run off with her. And it's entirely my own stupid fault.

***

Of course the train had left in the meantime. I wasn't even sure whether I still wanted to take it. What would be the point? She'd gone off without me.

I had plenty of time to think about it, because that had been the last train of the afternoon, and the next one was the night train at eleven o'clock. So I was stuck in Bergen anyway, no matter what I wanted to do. I deposited our bags in the left luggage lockers at the end of the platform and trudged off into town to have a think. In a quarter of an hour I was down by the harbour, next to the fish market. Despite my bad mood - and who could blame me for that? - I couldn't help noticing what a beautiful setting it was. In front of me, the harbour protected by the archipelago of rocky islands and behind, the densely forested Mount Fløien and other mountains hemming in the plain on which the town was built. What now?

I'd made my mind up by the time I'd got through a few cans of the local Hansa beer and a double portion of Norwegian fish and chips from the open-air market. Yes, I'd made my mind up that I would never be moving to Norway if beer cost that much. Even if the beer had a German-sounding name because of Bergen's former status as a member of the Hanseatic League of merchant ports, the prices were definitely Norwegian rather than German.

I'd also decided to press on to Oslo and try to find them at the Viking Ship Museum. I bought myself a cabin for the trip on the sleeper to Oslo, but I stayed up a good part of the night in the bar with the panoramic windows, turning over the events of the last few hours around in my head while watching the fabulous scenery scroll by. This is after all one of the most famously spectacular railway journeys in the world, and with good reason. The glimpses down into fjords, the upland plateaux with their placid, clear mountain lakes, the rushing, tumbling, white water in the streams and springs, the jagged mountains, the rocky outcrops, it was all there laid out before me. Just like Max had said. It was not long since midsummer's night and we were not all that far from the land of the midnight sun, so it never really got dark. Even if the sun did disappear from view for a couple of hours, we remained in crepuscular light. Easily enough to become bewitched by the steep uphill climb through the mountains around Bergen and up to Myrdal. Here was the junction with the famous Flåmsbana railway ride, which winds twenty kilometres steeply down to the little village of Flåm at the head of the next fjord. This time I wouldn't be taking it, but I vowed to return another time, hopefully in happier circumstances. And just before, we had passed through Voss, one of the stops I thought Linn and I would be making to see the Norwegian cup and ring markings. But this would have to keep till some other time too.

As we passed the halfway point at about three o'clock, fatigue overtook me and I side-slipped and staggered my way down the swaying corridor to my berth to sleep out the rest of the journey until woken by the cabin attendant with a cup of tea for an early breakfast. I was glad that the train had been fairly empty so I hadn't had to share a cabin. I think I would have been far from anyone's idea of an acceptable travelling companion, lurching noisily in at three o'clock, and spending the remainder of the night tossing and turning, belching, and worse, far worse.

It was still only six-thirty when we arrived at Oslo Central Station, but I jumped straight into a taxi and told the driver to take me to the Viking Ship Museum. Linn and Max were hours ahead of me but I thought they'd be turning up at the Museum at opening time, and I wanted to be there and ready for them when they arrived. It turned out to be about twenty minutes or so outside the city on the Bygdøy peninsula, looking back over the water to the harbour of Oslo. It was a bit chilly out in the early morning air and I was glad when the time got round to nine o'clock and the very friendly staff opened the doors to their first customer of the day. Their response to my question about the prehistoric rock art exhibition was unexpected to say the least. They had never heard anything about it! They were very nice about it and rang around to all the other museums which might have been organising such an exhibition, and even tried the tourist information and the university archaeology department, but drew a total blank. I didn't know what to think. Had Linn and Max been in on something together? Or had Max taken us both in? Or? I couldn't work this out at all. I'd been well and truly had, one way or another.

Max had said the Professor was providing the exhibits, hadn't he? Maybe he could shed some light on this, I thought in desperation. I fumbled with the buttons on my mobile, hoping that I had kept his home number in its memory from when we'd rung him from Bratislava to let him know how the conference had been going. For once, luck was on my side. Taking the risk that he might still be in bed - after all we were one hour ahead in Norway so it was still only about half-eight and the Prof was not a morning person - I dialled his number, if it is indeed possible to 'dial' using push buttons.

A croaky voice answered after a long wait.

"Dodd, you realise it is very early, do you not?"

"I do, Professor, and I apologise, but it's an emergency."

"But I told you yesterday - no, it's now the day before yesterday, in the evening - there is no exhibition! Didn't Linn say?"

"What? You mean Linn phoned you already?"

"Yes, from the ferry. While you were sailing over to Bergen. I don't know what Max is up to, but he is, as you say so nicely, pulling both of your legs, and Linn's too."

"I just don't understand, Professor. Have you any idea what's going on? Has Linn phoned you since then? The problem is she has gone off with Max and I've no idea where they are."

"This is most strange. I've heard nothing more since her short call when she told me that you were going to this non-existent exhibition and on a trip to look around the rock art sites of Hordaland. And about Max - I wonder what's going on with Max - he's a good student. He really has an in-depth knowledge, a bit like Linn, a kind of empathy with the people of prehistory. This is all very confusing, Dodd."

"It certainly is, Professor. I don't know what we can do. She's not answering her phone, not to my calls at least. I have to admit we've had a bit of a row and she's run off with Max. Though why she should do that when she knows he's a liar is beyond me. I haven't had time to work that one out yet. I'll be back in touch, Professor. And if Linn contacts you again, please let me know."

"I will do, Dodd, I will. And good luck. Come and see me when you return. Please."

"I shall, Professor. Thanks for your help."

CHAPTER TWELVE – RE-UNITED

I go in to seek help, to report a missing person, to do my civic duty. But I come out feeling as if I'm guilty of withholding information, of delaying an inquiry, of a crime, even. I realise those detectives and their psychologist Doctor Ingram were only doing their job the best way they see fit, but when you're not used to it...

And the other trouble is, overhearing their conversation about Linn and psychosis has got me worried. I know nothing about mental illness. Unless you count what I vaguely recall from watching the news or crime programmes or 'One flew over the cuckoo's nest'. It's never impinged upon me personally – I don't think any of my friends or family have ever been affected by it. Though how would I have been able to tell anyway? But now I begin to think back to things that Linn did and things that she said, in her waking time and in her dreams, and I can tick them off against my mind's amateur psychology checklist. I'm torn four ways between defiant denial that Ingram could be right, realisation that his diagnosis might explain a lot about Linn's behaviour, feeling sorry for Linn, and feeling sorry for myself, as in what have I got myself into? And feeling guilty, which is the worst of all. Make that torn five ways.

After all, I'd already started trying to analyse Linn, hadn't I? Remember when I was watching her dreaming on the ferry and wondering whether I was myself being drawn into a waking dream? And I have been secretly recording her talking in her sleep with a view to sending a tape to my linguist friend at Durham University. Though I never actually got around to making a tape. But this is no good, is it? I need a break from all this thinking and worrying, a chance to escape again.

Saturday afternoon in the Toon and I'm wandering aimlessly, mulling these thoughts over. They'd kept me awake all night too. I catch my first sight of the black and white hordes surging out of the Central Station in their fortnightly friendly invasion. They'll be heading for favourite pre-match watering-holes in the Bigg Market and other hives of activity all around the Toon.

That trip up to Lordenshaw after the grilling in the police station yesterday did me some good. A breath of fresh air to clear the head, but maybe a bit of stale air would not go amiss now. Plenty of bars to choose from for that, for sure.

I turn up Collingwood Street 'that's on the road to Blaydon', past the old grey Barclays Bank branch with the rounded entrance which stood at the corner of the street for years on end. It's now a vodka bar, and probably makes more money that way than the bank ever did. At the end, I look up at the site of the long-since-demolished old office where my granda used to work at Number One, Collingwood Street, opposite Saint Nick's Cathedral. My dad told me how my granda took him up the narrow spiral stairs to the top floor window to see the start of the 1962 Blaydon Races centenary parade. I hope there'll be one in 2012 so I can go to the top floor somewhere and look down too. God willing.

Then over the road and into the Bigg Market. And into Balmbra's, which has always been one of my favourites. I couldn't resist it. 'I took the bus from Balmbra's' – it's where the Blaydon Races was first performed. Memories of more recent Thursday nights with local bands in the old Music Hall at the back.

"A pint of Ex and a packet of pork scratchings please, pet."

Out into the light and there's Lord Harpole's hottest curry in the world upstairs in the Rupali; Newgate Street and Supermac's boutique; the number thirty-three trolley buses that took the schoolkids down Grainger Street to the station; the Grainger Market and Robinson's bookshop, goldmine for Biggles, Jennings and William books; and the Handyside Arcade.

The Handyside Arcade? Yes, I fancy a walk around the sloping floors of the little old arcade. I haven't been for years. The last time, it had been a refuge for all aspects of the Geordie alternative lifestyle. Just before I left to work on the continent, they were going to knock it down and build another soulless shopping mall extension, but there was such an outcry that they made it into a Grade II listed building. My great grandfather Bill had a locksmiths business there. It's a great place.

But before that, I'll just pop into my favourite greasy spoon café at the bottom end of the Grainger Market. There it stands, a monument to times gone by, all resplendent in red leatherette, cream-painted woodwork and aluminium fittings. I'm a bit peckish, which isn't surprising as I had no breakfast, just a Bodum of coffee, and now it's way beyond lunchtime. Hmm, I wonder if it's too late to ask for an all-day breakfast?

"Too late? Oh well, how about a bacon stotty sandwich, a couple of sausages, and a fried egg? That'll do canny."

"Oh, and a pot of tea, please. I'll be back in a minute – I'll just go and buy the Chronicle."

Just perfect - rashers of crispy bacon, lashings of melted butter oozing out the sides of the stotty and down your chin, crunchy-cased Cumberland bangers, a fully-fried fried egg with those crispy brown frilly edges, and a couple of mugs of tea.

A pair of young lads in Toon tops pop their heads around the café door and say we've won again, one-nil. At least things are looking good for some.

I'm not in the mood for celebration, but out of force of habit I head for the Newcastle Arms just across the street and up from the Back Page sports bookshop on Darn Crook as was, St. Andrew's Street as is. It's named after the oldest church in Newcastle down on the bottom corner of the street where it joins with Newgate Street. It's heaving as usual. The pub, not the church.

"Hello, Dodd! Haven't seen you in a while! You weren't at the match."

"No. I've been wandering around thinking about what happened to me yesterday. I was, as they say in police circles, detained."

"The poliss? What's up?"

"Oh, I've done nothing wrong, don't worry. I just went in to report a missing person. And now I think of it again, maybe you can help me. I don't think there's much chance of you knowing this, Ron, but did your sister ever mention a girl called Linn Rorting who might have been a couple of years or so younger than her at school?"

"Not that I can recall, Dodd, but I can ask Di for you, if you like. But it's a long time ago now."

"Did you say Di, Ron? I'd forgotten your sister's name, it's been such a while since I've seen her."

"Yes, Di, Diane if you prefer."

"Did she ever get married, then?"

"Yeah, a few years ago. To a pillock called Weetwood. I can't stand the feller. And neither can Di, as it happens. They're going through a really rocky patch. In fact they've to all intents and purposes broken up."

"It's a small world, Ron. I bet your Di works on organising field trips for local schools, doesn't she? And you know what? She hires my Linn now and then as the guide to show the kids around the historic sites."

"You're right! It certainly is a very small world. I'll try to give her a ring for you tonight, Dodd, and put you in touch."

"Well, it would be good if you could. You see, Linn sort of dumped me and disappeared all in one day!" I couldn't face telling him the rest of the story about the visit to the police station and the psychologist's diagnosis.

"I've been there too, marra! She'll turn up again, you'll see. But in any case I'll definitely ask me kid sister for you."

"Thanks, Ron. You never know, it might help. Anyway, enough of my troubles. Hoo's it gannin' for yee, Ron? What're ye having?"

"Oh cheers, can you get me a bottle o' dog? I'll save us a spot over by the entrance, there's nee place left to stand."

It took me five minutes to battle my way to the bar and back with our two pints of broon.

"By, it's stowed out! Here's your glass. So what have you been up to lately?"

"Actually I'm just back from Latzikunia. We're buying in pressed-steel body parts from them. Cheaper than making them ourselves now. All we do is the design and the fabrication of the tooling, and then we send the dies out to the factory there. We do the negotiations and the distribution logistics and they do the metalworking. They're good workers, the Latzikunians, and they cost a quarter of what we pay here. It leaves me with a guilty conscience, mind. But what can you do? I've got to balance me figures, otherwise I'm oot on me arse. But hey, honestly, it breaks me heart to see those lads oot there earnin' buttons. And riskin' tha' limbs, Aa can tell ye. There's nee such thing as occupational health and safety in Latzikunia, nee machine guards, nee safety interlocks, nee steel-capped boots, noot! Just geet huge presses on a beaten earth floor."

"Mind, that'll all change once they get inside the Common Market. What do you think of that?"

"Oh, I think they're going to let them in. It's true, ye knaa," his voice getting louder, maybe under the influence of the Broon, "they're lettin' the buggers in!"

At this very moment, a couple of very presentable lasses make their appearance on the threshold and flash us an accusing look.

"Sorry, we didn't mean yous two, pet! Come on in. No, it's the Latzikunians, like. They're letting them in, aren't they?"

"If you say so," the shorter one replied, with a puzzled smile.

"No really, I apologise. Can we buy yiz a drink to make up for it?"

"Go on then, thanks! Two Cuervo Gold margaritas please!"

"Oh, I don't know if they'll have them here, mind…"

"They do. We're regulars here, me and Melanie."

Another five-minute struggle through the serried ranks of black and white before I make it back. I have time to think while I'm waiting to get served. What did I come out for? Was it for something useful? Oh well, whatever it was, it can wait. Something more interesting to do now. Though my heart's not really in it.

"Cheers. I'm Joni by the way. Our mum and dad were hippies."

"Pleased to meet you. Has Ron told you my name's Dodd? Our mums and dads probably got our names out of a book, or off a map in my case."

"How do you mean?"

"I'm named after a mountain! Or at least a hill."

"Yer not!"

"I am! Look it up, Dod Law! Except they added an extra 'd' on."

***

Must have been something I ate. Or drank maybe. I was drowning, sinking ever deeper. Fast, like a dead weight in a dead sea. I was on my back and gazing up to the surface as the light receded fast. Then I turned, and it became a dive. When would I breathe again? Faster still as the water rushed past and enveloped me at the same time, welcoming me to its earthy womb with greater warmth the deeper I dived. From the initial blackness emerged gradually some shades of light and perhaps some figures deep down. And there she was swimming up towards me. Naked and beautiful. Gracefully approaching and our hands about to touch. But I had to turn back. She smiled a sad smile but with an expression of accepting as if to say maybe not this time, but soon. Soon. But I needed air and was struggling to get back to the surface. Intently I stared upward to the life-giving light. My lungs felt like they were about to burst when at last I broke through as if reborn.

Gasping, I almost jumped out of my bed. Sitting bolt-upright I took in air by the grateful lung-full before realising I actually needed some of that mineral water on the floor in front of the little bedside table to compensate for the cold sweat. As I stood up to go to the bathroom I squinted my eyes to make out the red numbers of the radio alarm clock telling me it was three-twenty in the middle of the night. With the window on tilt, the splish-splashing of a rainy night in Geordieland was clearly audible. On my way back to bed for the second half of a bad night's sleep I caught the sounds above the rain of a couple quarrelling four floors below. In the yellow glow of the street light I could clearly see her straggly rain-soaked hair. White blouse and miniskirt. No jacket on him either. Both drunk of course. Must have come up from the Quayside in search of a taxi. But there was one just driving past and splashing them generously from the kerbside puddle. The driver was obviously too wise a hand to want to take these two on board.

"It's aalways the same wi yee. Ya bliddy jealous. Aa divvent want noot te dee wi yee any more. Hadaway back to that slag ya married tee."

"Ah howay man, it waz aanly the drink taakin!"

I closed the window. Entertaining though it sometimes was, I didn't need any late-night-early-morning-reveller drama right now. Lying in bed, I gradually drifted off again, but this time without drowning. But also without finding Linn. Where was she? Is it possible to just disappear from the face of the earth? Of course not. Come back, Linn, please. What I wouldn't give to be having a row with you now, like those two down on the street. It would mean you were here. But you're not. We need to talk. I need to understand you. And to help you, if that's the way it turns out. And I miss you like hell. That's what this is without you: hell.

***

Six-thirty and Radio Newcastle was telling me the day would stay as wet as the night. Could have done with more sleep of course. How to focus on the day ahead with no Linn to look forward to in the evening? The rush-hour was a confusion of umbrellas and wet newspapers, getting on and off buses, with me finally plonking myself down to a desk whose telephone was already ringing in manic tones. The meeting went on through a standing coffee break, and the coffee was awful. Lunch time took an eternity to come round and just as I was taking my first bite into the pasty I had bought at Greggs between buses, the phone rang with even more urgency than it had first thing.

"You must come. You must. Now!"

"Why, Professor? What's happened? Has Linn got in touch, is that it?"

We had only spoken briefly on the day of my return from Oslo, promising to let each other know as soon as either of us heard anything from Linn.

"I must show you something. We have to go there today. It is very important. I have never seen anything like this."

"Go where? And why?"

"Up to Lordenshaw. There's something extraordinary."

"Professor, please, I have other things on my mind right now."

"No. We must. You are not understanding. There are new rock markings. They are from her. From Linn. Come. Get a taxi. Meet me outside the Haymarket. Now."

It took me a fair bit of time to square it with the boss. Whatever it was, my story must have been plausible. The taxi ride across the city centre was a rainy blur, played out to the beat of some bland mid-Atlantic garbage rock with the windscreen wipers completely out of synch but the more mesmerising for that. The conversation never got past the driver's opening: "Aa divvent think it's eva ganna stop. It's been stottin' doon aal mornin."

I had already fumbled to get the fare ready as I knew he couldn't stop for more than a couple of seconds right outside the Haymarket. Three pounds sixty. Here's four, keep the change. And already he was speeding off, indicating to turn right after the Dirty Angel and maybe on towards the Poly. The traffic was the usual lunchtime chaos. But no professor waiting outside the pub. He's not on the drink, is he? Was all this just the drink talking? Were both of us drowning men clutching at straws?

Two doors to choose from and I chose the wrong one. This was the bar. It was also a time-capsule, a Tardis in the middle of planet Newcastle. The hair, the beards and the leather jackets were straight out of the seventies, as were the sounds of Tull and Co straight out of the jukebox. Life was still a long song as I went back into the street and through the other doors into the lounge. Quieter here, lots of university staff and would-be intellectuals if it weren't for the effort involved. Ineffectuals, more like. Sat there at a little beaten-copper table in the far corner were the professor and a well-past-middle-age, white-haired and bearded colleague. A battalion of empty bottles bore witness to their cares of high office.

"Dodd. Good, here have you come at last. What has been keeping you? This is my friend, Slime."

"Pleased to meet you, er, Slime."

"Just wor little joke, man. I'm a senior lecturer in mining engineering, hence the acronym. I'm afraid I waylaid your Professor somewhat. I'm celebrating... well, me redundancy really, in good old North-East minin' tradition. Aye, the buggers hev made iz redundant like. Not many colliers left in collierland now."

The accent, like the patter, was unmistakably Ashington.

"Yes, I'm afraid we have had ourselves one or two bottles, and a couple of whiskeys. I have bought a half bottle to take with us. It is in my rucksack here, along with some overalls for the dig. It is going to be damp and dirty. We will need some Dutch courage, you will believe me."

I wasn't really sure what to believe now. All that urgency and yet he'd found the time for a mini lunchtime session in the Haymarket with his partner in, er, slime. Maybe I would need some Dutch courage. But for certain we needed some transport, as there was no way I was going to let the Professor drive. What we got was a Noda taxi with a Polish driver.

"From Cracow. Sorry my English not so very good, like."

But he was making great progress with his Geordie. We had been lucky enough to hail him at the bottom of Claremont Road, so he executed a neat U-turn by exploiting the entrance to the

University Theatre car park, and soon we were being whisked over several lanes of tangled urban motorway where it was impossible to tell which side of the road the British drive on, and Jerzy wasn't too sure in the first place. Thanks to our directions we were soon speeding along Gosforth High Street and within the hour we were in the wilds of Northumberland and only minutes from Lordenshaw in the still-pouring rain.

The Professor told me he had taken pictures but his digital camera had then been stolen in the crowds at Monument Metro station. And anyway it was better I should see these markings for myself. His hesitation to talk in the taxi was quickly dispelled by Jerzy's somewhat limited repertoire. By the time we reached the turn-off to Lordenshaw the meter said thirty-five pounds. We paid, and Jerzy agreed to switch it off on the strength of our assurance that he would also have our fare back to Newcastle.

Huddled under the Professor's oversize black and white umbrella, we changed out of our clothes and into the overalls, and with me carrying his clinking-clanking rucksack, we squelched our way across the field and up the slope of the hill-fort. Added to the downpour was a gusty Northumbrian wind. Visibility could have been better. The Professor pointed to a large rock at the edge of the fort, skirted by still lush bracken and wild grass. Even in the mud around them I could make out the marks of recent activity.

It was our rock, Linn's and mine. But it had changed – it was as if someone had seamlessly joined the lost half that Linn and I had discovered in the cave onto the existing half.

"I am simply incapable of understanding it, Dodd. It just wasn't like this before. This rock is twice as big as it was. We've got records of it. There are powers at work here, Dodd. Mark my every word."

I put his talking in riddles down to the drink. He took a nip from the whiskey bottle he had asked me to take out of the rucksack's outside pocket.

Our boots and overalls were by now covered in mud. And as we parted the undergrowth with the aid of the umbrella, we were quickly soaked through.

"There, you see now?"

"See what?"

"The markings from one rock continue across and match up exactly with the markings on the other. It's like two giant jigsaw pieces which finally have been put back together."

With the index finger of his right hand he traced the lines of some very faint markings low down in the rock. It could have been any old scratching, really. But next to the figure, more straight lines - but arranged in what could conceivably be construed as writing, child-like, unaccomplished, maybe also no more than random scratchings. Time-worn, they were indistinct. But when you looked long and hard enough at them, you could just about make out what looked like a word. Could my eyes really see the word 'LINN'?

It was as if the world had stopped turning and then suddenly gone into reverse. The past leapt forward, skipping over the millennia, and the rain kept falling. Looking around me, at the rock and its ancient cup and ring markings, through the drenching rain and the tears streaming down my face I felt... I don't know what. Her presence, maybe? Their presence?

"It's a hoax," I said. "Somebody's idea of a sick joke."

I said this just to say something, anything. But secretly my mind was racing, wondering how on earth Linn had managed to transport the rock we had found back up here to the top of Lordenshaw and even more, weld it back together into a single massive stone. It was beyond mortal comprehension. What's more, it was beyond rational explanation, I thought. And for this, I wasn't sure whether I was relieved or disturbed. Relieved because maybe it told me that Linn was back. Or disturbed because the explanation that I could imagine for all we had seen was, like I just said, beyond rational explanation.

I wasn't convinced that the markings really did say 'LINN'. But was it not too much of a coincidence for the markings to look so much like her name, yet still be something else? Then again, if she really had come back, would she not at least have contacted me, if only to say goodbye? On the other hand, when we'd gone back together to look for our find, hadn't she been as shocked as me to find the rock had disappeared from its hiding place in the cave? Or was she that good an actor?

The rock was now back in its original resting place, for this it undoubtedly was. Though there was nothing conclusive to say that it was Linn who had been the one to bring it back. Even if her words on finding the stone had made it clear that this was precisely her intention.

"We must take photos again. I have another camera. In my rucksack. You have seen it for yourself now. Seeing is believing, that's what you say, isn't it?" Another sip of whiskey. "Zis is, I think, enough for you, how you say, to take on board the ship for one day."

We squelched our way back out of the fort, down the slope and across the field. And waiting for us in the car park were tyre tracks in the mud. Jerzy had turned and gone. No return fare to Newcastle. Had he received a better offer, out here in the wilds? It was a good hour's walk to Rothbury, where the Newcastle Arms kindly let us shower and change out of our dig overalls in one of the rooms. After an early-evening meal and no more drink, the Professor was just about sober. This time the taxi fare was fifty-five pounds.

CHAPTER THIRTEEN – FIVE BRIDGES

I hardly slept that night. What to make of the new find? I was now conditioned to consider all possible explanations, logical, illogical, rational, irrational, mortal and immortal. Something had been gnawing away at my memory since seeing Linn's name carved into the rock, like her signature on a work of art, but my synapses just couldn't make the final connection. You know how it is sometimes when a thought springs into your head while you're engaged in doing something else and you say to yourself that you'll just finish what you're doing and then go back to the idea. But when you finish, you've forgotten. Then you wrack your brains trying to bring back whatever the hell it was to your prime consciousness.

The light was already streaming in through the wide-open window and I gave up on any further attempt at getting to sleep. I pulled on my running shorts and trainers, hung the door key on its ribbon around my neck and hit the streets. I've always found running is a good accompaniment to thinking things through. The rhythmic pounding of your soles on the pavement, your breathing providing another rhythm out of tempo with the first, and your heart yet another. After a mile or so you reach a steady state, where you don't need to think consciously about the physical effort of the running. A kind of euphoria which frees and expands your mind from the everyday to where you need to be.

And that is how it came to me as I crossed over the Tyne on the High Level Bridge. Something that Bulgarian twat of a student had said. About how some prehistoric people believed rocks were the gateway to another world. Like a moment of epiphany.

I'm not a believer in any of those kinds of things. But it would be an explanation, wouldn't it? Linn had finally succeeded in her quest to find the missing half of her rock, she'd pieced it together and perhaps somehow this had unblocked the gateway to enable her to return to some other world. Am I going crazy? Thinking these kinds of things? Or maybe I am becoming a believer. But doesn't there have to be a practical explanation too?

What would that Doctor Ingram make of me in this state? I bet he'd love to get me on his couch, if it's true that psychologists really have such things. Or is it psychiatrists who do that? I suspect it is. I really need to get onto the Internet, or maybe the good old local telephone directory might be better to help me find someone who can explain to me some of the basics about mental illness. Maybe someone involved in a charity or a helpline, rather than a psychologist or psychiatrist. Someone down to earth who can help me understand what Ingram meant when he was talking about a psychosis. But with all that's been happening, I simply haven't had a spare moment. Okay, I know I didn't have to get myself drunk on Broon on Saturday afternoon and evening, and then on through Sunday, sitting out on Linn's balcony drinking hot port and watching the Quayside market crowds stream past below, but it seemed a very good idea at the time.

I tumbled these questions and turned these thoughts around in my head as I criss-crossed the Tyne on my favourite training route. The Five Bridges. I warm up as I stretch my legs and bounce down the Hanover Street bank. The long stretch up river to the Redheugh Bridge gives you time to settle into the rhythm before the exhilaration of your first crossing of the river. Then it's back down into Gateshead and across Robert Stephenson's High Level Bridge. Turn right at the Cathedral and along Mosley Street and onto the Tyne Bridge to Gateshead, just like in the Great North Run. Down the bank past the Sage building for the final circuit: over the Millennium, up to and over the Swing Bridge, back to the Millennium and the return trip into Newcastle and the home stretch along the Quayside back to Hanover Street. It's hard work, mind, with all those ups and downs along the way. Life's like that. But there are plenty of options to take short cuts on days when you're too tired. Or to go further when you're breezing along. Life's like that.

Key in the door and still no solution, but plenty more questions. For a couple of hours I didn't know what to think, much less what to do. I switched on my PC and made some desultory attempts to look into prehistoric cults and beliefs. Mostly the articles were written by nutters. That's the trouble with the Internet – you hardly ever get a photo and an unbiased biography of the author. So you can easily waste your time reading guff uploaded by bearded, pony-tailed, sandal-wearing, white-socked weirdoes. The kind you wouldn't give the time of day to if they started giving their opinions to you face to face.

Then I moved on to a Google search on Ingram's word, 'psychosis'. I'd been putting it off, but I needed to face up to it. There were plenty of hits, more than six and a half million of them, four times as many as for 'prehistoric cults'. Surely that must be more than one per person suffering from this kind of disorder. It's as if there are more people interested in writing about it than there are people actually with the illness.

But hold on. Even a cursory glance at a couple of websites informed me that there are a lot more people than I would have ever guessed who will at one time or another in their lives have had some form of psychosis. Maybe even me. Or you. A disturbing thought, isn't it? And that was even before I knew what it really meant. The website of the Institute of Psychiatry at King's College

London says that one in twenty-five people will be afflicted by some form of psychosis during their lives. That means about two and a half million people in the UK alone. Or presenting it in a way that is easier to envisage, at least one person in your old school class, or your office, or the pub, or on the football or cricket pitch. The referee or umpire probably, lots of people might say! Or the bone-crunching central defender or the demon fast bowler, more like!

I picked up the local telephone directory from off the floor under the desk. I knew that they gave telephone numbers for all kinds of helplines in the front section.

"Can I come in and see someone? I'm worried about a friend."

"Our doors are open. You'd be very welcome, er…"

"Dodd, my name's Dodd. But it's not me, it's for a friend. She might have a mental problem."

"You're welcome to come round any time, Mr. Dodd. Now, if you like. Our office is in Shieldfield, on City Road, just up from the Quayside."

"I'll be there in five minutes. I'm just around the corner from you. That's why I chose your number to ring."

And in not much more than five minutes I was there and shaking hands with Clara, a tall, sturdy woman with a warm handshake, a broad, friendly smile, and an easy manner. Just the kind of person you'd hope to meet if you really were in trouble and needed a friendly stranger to confide in.

"So how can I help you, Dodd? Sorry, on the phone I just assumed it was your surname. You say you have a friend in trouble?"

"Well, it's like this. I have a friend who has disappeared and the police psychologist says she has a psychosis. The thing is, I don't know what he means. Can you tell me? You see, to me, she doesn't seem mentally ill... you know: depressed, or dangerous, or anything like that. For certain, she's got a fertile imagination, like she's living in a dream sometimes. And dreams, yes, she has some vivid experiences in her dreams. Talking in foreign languages and so on. But she's just as entitled to have her imagination and her dreams as anyone else, isn't she? So I wouldn't say she's mentally ill. Something else maybe, but not that. But I'm worried about her."

"Can I just ask you a question before we start, Dodd? I'm sorry, but you're not drunk, are you?"

"No, I'm not. I had one whiskey before I rang you. Some Dutch courage, you understand. But just one, and a small one at that. You can smell my breath?"

"Yes. It's just that more than half the people who come in here are either on the drink or on pills, and I was just wondering. It helps me to know who... to whom I'm talking!"

"Well I hope I've reassured you. No pills either by the way, ever. I've never felt the need. And I hope I still won't after what you have to tell me!"

"So let me start by describing to you what psychosis means, Dodd. It's a condition of the mind where the affected person is unable to distinguish between real events and imaginary happenings that they generate within their own mind. The real and the imaginary appear to them to be equally valid and real. The good news is that quite often these episodes of psychosis only last for a very short time, possibly only a few hours or days, weeks or months, and then the person makes a full recovery."

"So it's not a permanent thing. Like, you can snap in and out of it?" I ventured.

"Sufferers can be overloaded by too much information or overwhelmed by too much going on around them. This can lead them into strange kinds of behaviour. Or in other cases it can drive them to seek peace and quiet in a place of calm and solitude."

I thought of Linn's, and my own, attraction to Lordenshaw.

"Others can exhibit obsessive or repetitive behaviour. For instance repeated listening to loud music."

I wondered if that could extend to playing the same piece of pipes music to themselves over and over again.

"Hmm, possibly…" mused Clara, "and not just music. An affected person may occasionally begin to talk in a strange way…"

"Maybe like the foreign languages I told you about?" I asked. I'd of course immediately thought of Linn's strange languages.

"Yes, maybe, or a different voice, not their normal voice... By the way, how old is your friend?"

"Oh, she's in her mid-twenties."

"Exactly the age where psychoses are most common. Interesting..."

Clara then asked me to go over the questions that the psychologist had asked me, and I gave her some rather more honest and complete replies.

"Well, Dodd, he asked you all the typical questions that a psychologist would ask if he were diagnosing a case of psychosis. And to be frank, the answers you gave fit the picture rather well. Almost a textbook case actually. So it could be that she is suffering from some form of psychosis. It sounds as if it has been a persistent problem for a number of months or even years, so it may possibly even be schizophrenia. Mood swings, somewhat obsessive behaviour, mixing reality and imagination... The thing is though, you can have similar kinds of behaviour, and still live a perfectly normal life the vast majority of the time."

"Schizophrenia? That sounds terrible," I shuddered.

"All is not as black as it seems. She may not be schizophrenic at all. It's not certain. And besides, people can recover, though it can take months or years of gentle treatment and care. But the first thing is to find her before we can do anything to help her. You say she's back in the region. Let's hope she makes contact with you again soon."

"Yes, let's hope." The more I heard, the more worried I got about Linn.

The trouble was, my fevered imagination allowed me to fit something or other Linn had done or said, even if only once or in passing, to nearly every single symptom of psychotic behaviour that Clara gave. I even found myself thinking 'Hey, I do that now and again'. I was sitting there diagnosing myself as a psychotic too. Just like you hear about people who pick up a medical dictionary to have a quick browse feeling perfectly fine, and after a quarter of an hour they have to be helped to bed to recover from the onset of several grave afflictions.

So it was that after an hour or so spent with Clara at the helpline centre, I came out with a conclusion or more like a dilemma as I walked slowly back to Hanover Street. Had I got myself mixed up with a person, namely Linn, suffering from some form of psychosis, just as Ingram had diagnosed rather too glibly for my liking? And he would be quite likely to include the piper, maybe the professor, and maybe even me within his diagnosis too. Or... take a deep breath... there was a perfectly good, irrational, mystical, unreal explanation for all that had been going on. Rather spoiling the dilemma, there was also the possibility of a third alternative – a logical explanation. But I couldn't for the life of me see my way to it. Sooner or later I was going to have to choose.

I sat back down at my desk and shuffled the mouse from side to side to bring my PC back to life. The same thoughts were still going through my mind when up popped a message - 'A new e-mail has arrived'. It was from the Professor and read, 'Here attached are the new photos.' But there was no attachment. A minute or two passed and there was another message: 'Am realising I have made a mistake. But now here they are.'

And this time they were there. The first a general view of the site taken from about ten metres or so back, revealing nothing but a large rock in a field somewhere, overgrown with bracken and weeds and surrounded by muddy footprints.

The second, however, was a close-up. At 80% the marks were barely legible, so I blew the picture straight up to 150%. The rune-like characters we read as 'LINN' were open to various interpretations. A random chiselling of crude lines was one of them. If the two lines of the L were any closer together, they could be read as a 'less than' sign. We were clutching at straws really, wanting to believe in something that was impossible, beyond the realms of earthly experience. We were as crude and as base as early man worshipping the sun, the moon and the stars. Perhaps these lines represented patterns that Neolithic man had perceived in the clear Northumbrian night sky, linking up the stars showing him the way. The cups and rings too, perhaps. All just vague and ignorant imaginings of higher powers guiding and commanding them, leading them to carry out sacrifice and never-ending battle with their fellow, ignorant and abysmal man, and nature itself.

Then out of idle disappointment I clicked on the 1500% button, the highest possible resolution on my PC. It gave a grainy image of one corner of this gravestone-like rock. And the grainy pixels seemed to form a shadowy pattern. Taking it down to 1300, the image seemed to be part of a face. And at 900, Linn was smiling her sad smile at me and I thought I was going out of my mind.

The phone rang.

"Hello?" I never give my name. A while ago – oh, long before all this started - I had a spate of anonymous phone calls where whoever it was, or whoever they were, waited until I gave my name and then put the phone down without saying anything. I felt as if I was giving them the advantage – they knew my name, but I didn't know theirs. So I decided to only ever say hello and nothing else. You wonder if they're checking to see if you're in. Maybe they're going to come round and burgle you if you don't answer. Or maybe they just want to frighten you. Or maybe it's just a joke. It's not a nice feeling. But a voice comes through this time:

"Hello? Dodd? This is Di Weetwood."

"Di! Ron told you. I was hoping he would. Thanks for phoning. I'd really like to meet you and have a chat. About Linn."

"Yes, that's what Ron told me. Well if you like, we could meet now. I'm just finishing work, and I can be in the town in half an hour."

"That would be great. How about we meet in the Cooperage? Ron and I used to go to the upstairs room to see the local bands there years ago."

"I remember - I went along lots of times too, you know. I'll see you there. I am sure we'll be able to recognise each other, even if it is ten years, at least, since we last met!"

She hadn't changed much. She still looked great. We settled down over a couple of pints of Bass and then a couple more as we reminisced over old times before cutting to the quick.

"You went to the police to report Linn missing and told them that she was seeing someone, a stranger she'd only just met. They gave me a rough time, you know!"

"Oh, Dodd, I had no idea that you were Linn's mystery man! She never went into details, not even your name. She's a bit of a dark horse, is Linn."

"That's half the trouble isn't it? Nobody knows much about her. She appears into your life, lights up all around her, then disappears into thin air."

"Same at school. She wasn't with the rest of us from the start. She joined in maybe the third year, was only there for three years or so, then dropped out. You won't have heard what she was like in history and literature lessons - she was so funny - apparently she kept telling the teachers that they were wrong, that things didn't happen like that. You could say she was a bit disruptive, really. She was always getting detention. And then one day she just dropped out - no warning, just didn't come back. I didn't see her for years after that until she came to our office and registered with us to do her guided history tours."

"I get the feeling you don't know much more about Linn than I do."

"Like I said, she's a dark horse. A good friend, easy to talk to, but she doesn't let on much about herself. You never really know what she's thinking."

"I'm going to ask you an odd question - do you think that she could be a bit... disturbed? You know... nuts, or something? It's what I overheard the police psychologist saying..."

"Is that what they think? No. I wouldn't say that. But what do I know about such things? Nothing."

"You and me both, Di..."

"I don't think either of us are going to come out of this any the wiser, are we, Dodd? We're just going to have to hope that she turns up again of her own accord. We've got nothing to go on."

"Nothing at all. You know, I've just been to a psychiatric help centre a few minutes' walk from here in Shieldfield to ask some more about what it might mean, what the police psychologist was talking about. The lady there was very patient and helpful. The trouble is, based on what I could tell her, she thinks that Doctor Ingram could be right - that Linn's possibly suffering from some psychosis, as he called it, even schizophrenia. And obviously what you were able to tell Ingram tied in with what I said very well."

"He was nice, wasn't he? Doctor Ingram, I mean. Charming. And very professional. And very understanding."

"I didn't much care for him, myself, actually... But I suppose he's probably good at his job. It's just that I don't want to believe what they're saying about Linn. There's got to be another explanation... Diane, do you er... believe in... I don't know how to describe what I'm thinking of... you're going to think I'm nuts too!... reincarnation and the like?"

"How d'you mean, Dodd? You don't mean to say that you think Linn is reincarnated, do you? Goodness me!"

"I knew it! I shouldn't have mentioned it. It's only that it sort of explains everything. A few months ago, I would have laughed off any suggestion of the like. But now... I've got to admit, at the risk of whatever you might think of me, that I'm starting to think it might just be possible! Of course, I couldn't tell the police or the helpline people, otherwise they'd be carting me off too, wouldn't they!"

"Well, your secret's safe with me, Dodd! I won't be turning you in... I'll even sit with you a bit longer. I've never been for a drink with a mystic before! Can you magic up an Irish coffee for me? It'll set me up for the trip home - Irish coffee for Dutch courage!"

"Of course, Di! Two Irish coffees coming up - perfect for getting in touch with the spirit world, eh? The beer, wine and spirit world at least! Oh aye, and you don't need to tell Ron, do you?"

"Like I said, I'm the soul of discretion, me!"

"And we can keep in touch, can't we, Di? About Linn, I mean."

"Why aye, Dodd, man. Send us a message with your ouija board any time you like! No, but seriously, you'll be the first I'll tell if she contacts me, and I hope you'll do the same for me."

CHAPTER FOURTEEN – A SPLASH IN THE TYNE

"And now the late evening news from Look North. Northumbria Police are asking the public for any information which could help them in their enquiries to identify the severed head found hanging at Winter's Gibbet near Elsdon in North Northumberland earlier today. The familiar landmark of the replica wooden head was found by maintenance workers to have been substituted by a tarred leather casing within which was hidden a real human head. Viewers of a nervous disposition should turn the sound down and look away for the next few moments while we show a retouched photograph of the face of an unknown man thought to be in his early twenties."

I couldn't get to the remote control in time and caught a glimpse of the face and stood transfixed for what seemed an eternity. It was Max. I was sure of it. A death mask of Max. Whatever he'd done, I didn't wish that on him.

"Police suspect foul play. Anyone with any information should contact Detective Inspector Breamish of Northumbria Police at the following number..."

'Suspect foul play', eh? The sub-editor is going to get a rocket for that one!

What should I do? It's even Breamish who's dealing with it. I wonder if they've made the connection with Linn and what I told them? No, it can't be. Otherwise they wouldn't be asking for help to identify Max.

But what does this mean? Max has been murdered. Linn was the last person seen with him. They've both since disappeared. The police expert thinks Linn's psychotic or schizophrenic. The helpline lady just reinforced what Ingram said. It all fits together too well. But I don't believe it. I don't want to believe it. But not to believe it means believing in the unbelievable. But I've just seen the unbelievable, haven't I, up on Lordenshaw: me and the Professor standing under the drenching rain in front of the two halves of rock which had somehow been re-united after almost two thousand years. What to make of all this? Do I have to go and tell the police? Even if it means betraying Linn? I do, don't I? Then another thought struck me: Linn might also have been murdered at the same time, but they just haven't found her yet. That was too much to contemplate.

I had to get out of the flat. It was getting on for eleven in the evening. The shower had stopped and it was turning into a warm late-summer night.

The young ones along the Quayside this weekday evening were dressed to take full advantage of what could always be the last of the good weather. The clickety-clack of high heels was everywhere, wrapped in a cloud of assorted perfumes and aftershave. Bands of lads in shirt-tails trying to look cool. Groups of Barbie dolls with Byker accents encouraging them. The designer youth of the Now Society on a night out in its never-ending, never-satisfied quest for instant everything – but discardable, please, no questions asked, in the morning.

I needed a stiff drink, but not down here. Somewhere quiet. Even quieter places would still be open under the new licensing laws, at least those not too far from the city centre. A stiff uphill walk before the stiff drink, and the Printer's Pie answered my prayers. Upstairs may have been heaving but the bar downstairs was only half full, and the clientele comprised mainly Journal and Chronicle workers, journalists and printers alike.

Standing, almost cowering really, at the far corner of the bar, given a respectful space by the regulars and looking every bit the off-duty coppers they were, were DI Breamish, or Beamish or whatever he was called, and his sergeant. Of all the times to run into them, when they must be mulling over the severed head mystery. Just my luck. Mind, there's no reason why they should make any connection between the head and Max or Linn. No reason for them at all. It's too early for me to talk to them.

In any case there's nothing to say that I've even heard about the severed head - it's only just been on the late news, and I could have been out all night for all they know.

They saw me of course, and lifted their heads in recognition. But they didn't approach me. That could wait. He was going nowhere, they probably thought. A pint of McEwans lager and two double Tullamore Dews later and I was out again in the evening air, feeling the better for it.

Not trusting my detective friends that thoroughly, I made a long detour by walking up Pudding Chare alley to the Bigg Market and along to Grainger Street through the sizeable crowd of revellers even on this mid-week night. Then down to the Central Station, along Collingwood and Mosley Streets and hesitantly through the Pilgrim Street roundabout underpass, always a bit of a dodgy place, with a view to crossing the Tyne Bridge, looking blue and illuminated and splendid before me. I thought I would cross it, go down by the Sage – slug or whale, take your pick – and back over the egg-slicer Millennium Bridge and up to Hanover Street. Re-tracing the last stretch of my usual run, but at a much steadier pace tonight. That would surely tire me out enough for a good night's sleep at last.

Already as I set foot on the bridge the pandemonium in the middle was palpable. A police car with its blue light flashing. One officer talking to someone beyond the parapet while the other was radioing for assistance. By the time I got a third of the way across, a second blue flashing light had arrived and then a third, the last one being an ambulance. Gazing over to the left, the Sage was a blaze of light as crowds were streaming out after some concert or other. Beyond that, the Baltic gave a multi-coloured light-show that was celebrating its latest barely comprehensible exhibition. But never mind, the views from inside were always great.

Only ten yards away now and one policeman was asking pedestrians to cross please to the other side. The bridge had been closed to traffic. Must have been chaos on both sides. I could hear the potential suicide, I suppose that's what he was, shouting and bawling. Something about 'That lass, the stupid cow', and 'She'll have to wait for it, it's not the end of the month yet.' Must be about maintenance money or something. And 'The other one, she's just as bad… she won't have me back… says it's been too long… thousands of years, like… going off without a by-your-leave… who does she think she is? It's not as if it was my idea. I was just popping out round the corner. She should be happy to see me again, see I'm all right.' Bit of a slur with the drink. Par for the course for a late-night Tyne Bridge would-be suicide. I stopped short of where pedestrians were being moved to the other side and went to the parapet this side instead. In the dimness between two streetlights, I wouldn't stand out, and anyway, the officer had a steady stream of pedestrians to deal with. And they weren't all sober either, so he had his work cut out and wouldn't be bothering me.

After my eyes had adjusted to the lack of light down below, I could make out and hear what must have been, I suppose, a police launch. They were ready for all eventualities. I don't like to think about people drowning - there's something about the thought of dying in that way - knowing it's happening and being powerless to do anything to help yourself. The faces of my parents appeared, floating before my eyes. And then I heard our death candidate shouting at his new policemen friend and telling him he needed a piss.

He must have lost his tenuous grip on the parapet, or on life, or on both. The next thing I knew, there was a white splash in the water followed by darkness and screams from some of the Barbie dolls following events like me from a bit further back towards the Newcastle side.

The barge below suddenly lit up like a Christmas tree, two searchlights sweeping the spot where he had entered the water and likely resurfacing points. Seconds later and the chop, chop, chop of the police helicopter became audible, and the crackle of police radio seemingly everywhere.

A voice next to me said, "Aye, the currents ye knaa, tha treacherous aroond the bridges."

So how the hell did he know? There was quite a crowd gathered now. One man's death-wish had become a spectator sport.

The helicopter searchlight swept about wildly at first and then homed in on a splashing figure surprisingly far downstream so shortly after leaving the bridge. Heat-seeking technology - or could it have been a long-range breathalyser - must have helped them locate him that fast. More screams from the girls on the bridge.

"They'd better get him out quick. He cannit last lang in that", the voice next to me spoke again.

I turned my head towards my companion.

"How are you doing, Sergeant umm...?" I asked.

"Humbleton's the name. Oh, very canny, sor, thanks."

So it was 'Sir' now, all of a sudden.

"Busy at the moment?"

"Oh aye, sor, very busy. Working on a big case, we are. Gruesome. A severed head up on the moors, not far away from your Lordenshaw, akshully. At the old stob, ye knaa, Winter's Gibbett. It was going out on the late news tonight, but you've missed it now, I think."

"Sounds awful."

"And we're still looking at your missing person case too, of course, don't worry, sor."

"I wish you could find her, Sergeant."

"We're deeing wor best, sor."

The 'copter suddenly tilted to one side and to everyone's amazement. Then the tactic became clear. The downdraught was pushing the man towards the Newcastle side. Perfect entertainment for the crowd now gathered there too in front of the many establishments. And I could make out the flashing light of what had to be an ambulance winding its way around Sandhill bend at the bottom of Dean Street. The manoeuvre was working, and the splashing man was getting nearer and nearer the Quayside. The pilots must surely practise this, they couldn't possibly have thought it up on the spot, could they?

"They know they've got to be quick. The currents. If they didn't get him here, he'd be away past the Baltic in nee time. And deed. Even the strong swimmers. Bevvied up and fully clothed, and then the cold. Well..."

I could have done without the running commentary, really, but Sergeant Humbleton obviously felt we were on the same side, at least for the moment.

Then another splash, and another. My God, two people had jumped in from the Quayside.

"It's aal reet," the Sergeant assured me, "that's two o' wor lads. Thill hev 'm oot in nee time noo."

Despite my own intake, I could smell the drink on him without any problem. And his Geordie was the better for it. Two more minutes and some kind of cradle was being lowered down into the river. And then hoisted out again, more slowly.

"That's it. He's oot."

Two seconds later and there was a great cheer from the sizeable crowd on the Quayside. And then the bridge joined in. Another minute and the ambulance was speeding away back up Dean Street, light flashing. Gradually the crowds dispersed, and the police left, and traffic started to flow over the Tyne Bridge again. A pent-up mini rush-hour at first and then just a steady late-night mid-week trickle. Only the Sergeant and I were left leaning on the parapet.

"You wouldn't be thinkin' o deein' oot like that yasell, noo would yi, sor?"

"No, you don't need to concern yourself on my account. There've been enough drownings in my life. What will happen to him now?" I asked.

"Well if he's deed, they'll take him to the morgue in Heaton." Just a statement of fact, no emotion that I could detect.

"Oh, for Christ's sake. And if he's alive?"

"Nee need te take the Lord's name in vain, sor. It depends which side he jumped from."

"What?"

"Well it was a fairly central spot. But the lads will ev sorted oot whether it was Ny'cassell or the Gatesheed side. If it was Ny'cassell, they'll take him to Saint Nix in Gosfath in the mornin'. But it'll be the RVI forst, of course, to make sure he's okay. Physically like."

"And if it was the Gateshead side?"

My tone was exasperated.

"Not sure really. Still the RVI forst of course. And then some loony bin, near Saltwell Park Aa think it is. Not certain, though. Not my patch, you see." A belch. "Oops. Sorry."

"So to what do I owe the honour?"

"Well when we saw you in the Pie, me Inspecta thought it might be a good idea to see if you were, well, aal reet, ye knaa. You lost me very quickly and then Aa just went for a bit of a waak and seen this commotion on the bridge. And got lucky. You definitely weren't thinking of... yi knaa, yasell, wo yi?"

"Nothing could be further from my mind, I assure you." That was the second time he'd asked me! Was it genuine concern or just the drink making him forgetful?

"Well that's aal reet, sor, isn't it? Inspector Breamish asked me to say we'll be wantin' anotha little taak soon. Yi worn't plannin' on gannin' anywhere far soon, wo yi?"

"No. Am I a suspect or something?"

"Well not really, sor. Wi just thowt yi might be able to, well, help us wi wa enquiries, like, as they say."

"As they say."

"Aa'll be on me way, then. Gud neet, sor."

"Good night, Sergeant."

And off he walked, not the steadiest of off-duty walks, back towards the Newcastle side of the bridge and quickly out of sight. And that left me the only one leaning over the parapet and gazing into the waters of Tyne and the dancing reflections of the bridge lights. And the eddies and undercurrents swirling there in the cold just below me. There it was, the water of life and the water of death. Flowing steadily to the sea to evaporate into cloud and rain and wash down from the hills again in the never-ending cycle. There was only so much water, I supposed. And it got used time and time and time again. We were drinking the very same water our ancestors had drunk a thousand years ago. Two thousand, ten thousand years ago for that matter. It just went on being recycled. The water of Christ and the water of Mohammed. All part of the same mass, or Mass, even. From the sweat of the Caesars to the rain lashing down this afternoon on Lordenshaw. All one great pool. Like the gene pool of human life. And like time itself, with its own eddies, undercurrents and backwaters. Bits that had been forgotten, twisted, frozen, evaporated. Recycled. Yes, time itself was being recycled. I thought I understood that now. Or maybe it was just the whiskey, *uisce beatha*, the water of life, that helped me to understand it for the time being.

And our would-be suicide? Had he survived? Had he wanted to? Had he been reborn through a kind of baptism in the pagan waters of the river-god Tyne? Or was he lying now on a cold slab in Heaton morgue? It was half past three when I finally got back to the flat. I switched the radio alarm clock off. To hell with work. I would head off to Lordenshaw in the morning. Perhaps she would be there to meet me. Her presence was all I craved. If not, maybe it was time to bail out, before this whole house of cards came crashing down on me.

CHAPTER FIFTEEN – THINGS COME TO A HEAD

The same shudder traverses my whole body again as I drive slowly past Winter's Gibbet with the blue and white-striped police incident tape cordoning it off. This is the third day in a row I've been drawn up here. But it's the first time that I am the only one around, except for the watching police officer. The novelty must have worn off for the majority of the ghoulish onlookers, he must be thinking.

Bloody hell, he's taking down my registration number. Maybe he's recognised my car from the previous days. I'm going to have to go to the police now, before they call me in. I'm going to have to tell them that I've recognised the severed head as Max. It's going to be another case of them asking me, "Why didn't you come to report this earlier?" And what can I reply?

I'd better drive straight down there and explain myself before they haul me in.

"You're making a habit of this, Mr Law. Why didn't you come to report this earlier?"

It was Inspector Breamish asking the questions, with Sergeant Humbleton looking on. At least I was lucky that that Ingram feller wasn't on the premises today. But I thought I could detect that Breamish was looking at me extra carefully, as if he was trying to remember how to analyse my non-verbal signals like Ingram had described. I wonder whether I might just have a slightly better memory than Breamish, and I contemplate throwing in a few contradictory gestures at inappropriate moments to get him confused, I hope. The trouble is, if I don't remember right, I might send out exactly the opposite signal to what I'm intending. And if Breamish gets himself mixed up and misinterprets the signals, then I'm maybe going to be in a worse position anyway.

Breamish went on, "We were just about to call you in. One of our more observant officers noticed that your car had passed by the scene of the crime three days in a row and took down your registration number. We'd just traced the number to you a few moments before you arrived on our doorstep. So why were you up there at the Gibbett?"

"I was wondering whether I had really recognised the face from the newspapers. I'm not sure, but it could be the student who ran off with

Linn. I gave you his name the last time I was here, Max Thracoslav. Do you think it could be him?"

"This is news to us, sir. We will look into it. You don't have a photograph of Max do you?"

"No. Didn't you get one when you were investigating Linn's disappearance?"

"You like to ask questions, don't you, Mr Law? I recall from our last interview. Our enquiries did not get that far, I am afraid."

I wanted to say something but I bit my tongue.

"Well, I should think you should be able to get one from his university records in Bratislava. Maybe even from our university here. He was a visiting student at the Archaeology Department here a while ago. You could maybe check with their admin people."

"Sergeant - could you ask someone to get onto that right away, please?"

"Yes, sir, right away," replied Humbleton, standing up to leave.

"Thank you, Sergeant..."

I interrupted Breamish: "And what about Linn? Maybe something has happened to Linn too. They were together the last time anyone saw them."

"Now, Mr. Law. We are considering that possibility too. But you also realise that all this puts you in an awkward position. Let's review where you stand. One of the people you reported missing may have been found dead, if you're identification proves correct. While the other, Miss Rorting is yet to be found. And from what we have been told about her by Doctor Ingram, she may be a prime suspect if indeed Max has come to harm. You may not know this, though you may have had your own doubts based on what you told us last time, but we have reason to suppose that Miss Rorting's mental state may be less than stable. Perhaps you have considered this possibility yourself and this has stopped you from coming to report this to us until now?"

"Inspector, I don't know what to think. I still don't know if it is Max in the first place. And even if it is, I can't believe that Linn could have done such a thing."

"Of course, there is another possibility that would have prevented you from coming in to see us. Let me put a few suppositions together and present them to you so that you can give me your opinion. For instance, I could be thinking that you are yourself implicated in the disappearance of both Max and Linn. Though the reason why you would put one of your victims on public display eludes me for the moment. Perhaps you too are not of wholly sound mind."

"No, no! Inspector, I think you're going too far. And you're wrong anyway."

"Well, if I'm not right, I am still wondering why you are acting in this way. I think you are holding something back. You've been going to Winter's Gibbett for three days now, and no doubt you've been doing a lot of thinking in between. But you don't come to report this until you're spotted by one of our officers."

"I came of my own accord!"

"Ah, but I think you maybe realised that you had been spotted and thought it was better to turn up here before we came to fetch you."

"It's not that, no!" I slammed the desk. As the shock wave reverberated around the room, I looked into Breamish's eyes and realised that he was observing me. Observing my very non-verbal action. And drawing his own conclusion.

"I think we may need to ask you to stay and help us further... I am going to leave you in the company of one of our constables for some time, while I go and discuss some thoughts with my superiors. If you wish to tell us anything more, please signal it to my colleague. Good day, Mr Law."

Is this what they call 'helping police with their enquiries'? It looks like I'm stuck. If I try to explain anything more, they're definitely going to think I'm crazy. Sacred stones, Romans, temples... I don't have a chance.

***

Hours later and the door opens and Inspector Breamish walks in and switches on a light. It's already getting dark outside.

"Doctor Law, we have some surprising news for you. This is no longer a murder enquiry. You're free to go."

I have been promoted again.

"What's happened? I don't understand. Is it Max, then?"

"Questions... It turns out that your friend the Professor at the Archaeology Department in the university had already been contacted by our pathologists. The Professor has been helping with their analysis of the remains. The severed head is not Max. It is thousands of years old. As I said, you are free to go and we're sorry for having had to ask you to wait here so long. We are of course still doing all we can to locate your friends, Max and Linn."

I am speechless at the news. I was sitting here, convinced that a murder had been committed, that Max was the victim, and that Linn might have been the murderer, or herself also a victim. My head bulging with thoughts, I marched along Market Street and turned up Pilgrim Street, heading for the university. I'd parked my car up there anyway, but now I was going to find the Professor. As I guessed, he turned out to be in the museum, looking after his relics in the storeroom.

"Hello Professor."

"Dodd. I am so relieved to see you. So you already know about Max?"

"Yes. I've come straight here from the police station. Am I glad that you were asked to investigate! The head, you must have thought like me that it was Max when you saw it? I was certain it was when they showed it on the news. I didn't know what to do. I was so confused I didn't even think to talk to you."

"I do not often watch the news, Dodd, I'm afraid. Otherwise I could possibly have avoided that unpleasantness with the police for you. The first time I saw the head was yesterday when I was called upon by my colleagues from the pathology department. And I can tell you that I got as big a shock as you when I saw it, probably more because it was the real thing in front of my own eyes. For me, it was Max. I was on the point of telling the police myself."

"So it is?"

"I was convinced for some hours. But then we looked at the results of our analyses."

The Professor sat me down in front of a white shrouded object on the storeroom bench. It looked no different from the other shrouded exhibits that he'd shown us in the storeroom on our previous visit to the museum. That now seemed an age ago.

"I have the head right here. This head, and it is the Winter's Gibbett head, I assure you, is almost two thousand years old. We have performed a carbon dating test on it and the evidence is irrefutable. This is not Max, however much you or I might think it is he. Bearing in mind what we discovered about the sacred stone on Lordenshaw, I think both of us now have very open minds on the subject."

"But it is him, Professor, I'm sure. Can I see?"

"If you wish. I hope you are not squeamish. The head is remarkably well preserved."

And so saying, the Professor drew back the shroud. I was so taken aback by the perfect likeness that I did not have space in my mind to dwell on the macabre circumstances.

"I swear it's Max, Professor. You must think so too."

"I do. But the scientific evidence is overwhelming. This is an archaeological mystery, not a murder mystery. The police are no longer treating this as a murder enquiry. They are wondering whether it could be a theft from an archaeology museum or the looting of an archaeological site. I don't know how they are going to deal with it now. I am thinking that the head will be the subject of a display in our museum and not evidence in a murder trial now."

"Thank you, Professor. It's going to take me some time to work this out for myself. Probably an eternity."

"And for me too, Dodd. I just don't know what to think. You should also know that the DNA analysis shows that the remains are of probable Eastern European or Mediterranean origin. Ancient Greek or Thracian, for instance. Like Max. It would most certainly make it much easier if we heard from Max or Linn. That would remove some of the crazier notions from my head."

"And mine, Professor. Let's go for a drink."

"A fine idea, Dodd. Do you mind if I call up my old friend Slime?"

"Not at all. A third head would do no harm in this case. Or should I say a fourth?"

CHAPTER SIXTEEN – FULL CIRCLE

It was the night of the new moon. The first since Linn had disappeared. The first since the mad piper had disappeared. The first since the Professor had made his amazing discovery of the rock made whole again. The first since the discovery of Max's head, for I was still convinced that it was Max's, however old it was. The first new moon I wouldn't be spending with Linn.

I felt the draw of Lordenshaw stronger than ever before.

The sky was blue-black. So was my mood. I picked up my pipes from the corner where they had been lying and tentatively played the first notes of Linn's 'Longing is belonging' lament. It was too much. Gathering up the pipes and torch in our fur rug, I drove to Lordenshaw and climbed in pitch darkness up to the rock. I didn't bother to light the torch until I had spread out the fur rug which now barely covered half of the rock. Like Linn had shown me, I poured some oil into the deepest cup mark and lit it from the torch, which I then extinguished. I took up my position with my back to the rock and faced in the direction of the invisible moon in the cloudless sky where it obstructed the light from a million stars.

I played the notes of the unfinished lament over and over, returning to the beginning each time I reached the curtailed and unresolved last phrase, as tears welled up and the lump in my throat grew ever larger. Down below in the valley, the lights of the villages went out, just as they had done that first time, and the only light came from the flickering oil-cup and the brightest stars. One last time I would play the lament. I held the final note for four bars and imagined that the sound was being sustained not only by my pipes but by others. The sound grew stronger and new notes flowed into my ears, as if my mind was creating its own ending to the lament, without any effort on my part. I tried to play the new ending but it was too much for my unskilled fingers, though the notes went on in my head, and I played along with a simple accompaniment. It sounded so right.

I became aware that the squeezing motion of my right elbow on the sac was being impeded and I turned my head and found Linn and the old piper alongside me. I didn't jump. Somehow it seemed normal. Somehow I wasn't surprised. It was they who were playing the lament through from its beginning to its new end. I wasn't afraid. I was happy to be there, even in a dream. The ending was still more beautiful than the beginning, and it was in a state of bliss that I stood there playing alongside my companions.

"Is it really you, Linn?" I whispered.

"It is. And we are all back together at last. Charles here, as you sometimes call him, he's recovering from a very cold bath that he slipped into last night. But at least he kept his promise to me tonight. Like I did to him. And see the others too. Look around you."

And arranged around the circle of the stony walls, I could make out the familiar faces of other people I'd met on Lordenshaw these last few months, smiling in the flickering light from their torches. The old lady and Nell the dog, the Professor, and three school children from the school trip. Could they be the ones who'd found the Mithraic cave, I wondered. Though the young girl chased by the dog was missing. And Bulgarian Max.

"Where did you disappear to in Norway, Linn?"

"We drove straight back to the ferry and came back to Newcastle. What with the ferry coming in so late, it had to leave nearly straight away on the return journey. So Max and I only spent a few hours in Norway."

"And why did you come back so fast, Linn?"

"I phoned the Professor from the ferry on the night of the storm and he told me that there was no such thing as an exhibition in Oslo, and that he'd had no contact with Max recently."

"I know. I rang him too, but only after I'd trailed all the way to Oslo. I wish you could have told me."

"I had a very good reason not to tell you! I got onto the car deck as soon as they opened it up and I sneaked a look in the back of the van and you know what he had? Our stone. And you know only too well how he found out where it was. From you! When you went and shot your mouth off, bragging about your find on the Internet forum on rock art. Max was online at the same time as you and he couldn't believe his luck when you gave out the location. How could you have done such a thing? God, I was fuming at you. It served you right when I abandoned you high and dry on that Norwegian platform! And anyway I couldn't say anything in case Max twigged that I knew he had the stone."

"Aye, I regretted it as soon as I'd done it. And even more when we went back and the stone had disappeared. I didn't dare tell you what I'd done. I felt so stupid. I don't blame you. But why was Max so interested that he dropped everything and came over within hours and took the stone away?"

"Well, this is where it starts to get complicated. I could tell you that he was acting for a rich collector who pays bounty money for rare archaeological finds. It's a good explanation. I could tell you he was a bounty hunter and leave it at that, couldn't I? Or I could tell you he was a nutter. A nutter who was obsessed with Roman times and who imagined that one of his ancestors from Thrace was a Roman Centurion and a believer in the Mithras cult. A Roman soldier who had been part of the advance guard forging north into Northumberland in the late seventies AD. Who had led his men in a raiding party and come upon our stone and hacked it in half to take it away as a centrepiece for a Mithraic temple. Or I could tell you that he and that soldier were one and the same person."

"You could, and a while ago, I'd have believed your first explanation, and dismissed the last out of hand. But there have been too many things going on recently. I don't know what to believe. From where I'm standing now, I'd actually go for your last explanation, however crazy it sounds. After all, it's either that or there's a police psychologist who says you're psychotic, or maybe even schizophrenic."

"Oh, you're talking about Doctor Ingram. Di Weetwood told me about him. Quite full of himself, she said. Ridiculous, isn't it? I ask you, do I look psychotic, or schizophrenic?"

I didn't know what to say, knowing what I now knew - that psychotics and schizophrenics can look as normal as anyone else, and behave just like anyone else almost all the time. Maybe my head was telling me something - that qualifies me for a psychosis too, doesn't it - but my heart wanted to believe in Linn. My heart was winning.

"No, pet, of course not. Either that or you'd get my vote in the Miss Psycho beauty pageant, and that's for sure. So he's a Roman conscript from

Thrace who stole a sacred stone. But now you've got it back. So where's the Roman raider now? He's just about the only one not standing around the walls of this fort."

"Do you remember back in the Professor's storeroom, I told you that those Roman vandals had no right to take our stones and use them for their temples? That they should never have done that. Well, I could tell you that he's back studying in Bratislava. Or I could tell you that maybe he won't be finishing his PhD... Let's just say that the next time they take down the fake head encased in tarred leather from Winter's Gibbet, they're going to get a nasty surprise."

"But they already have! Have you not seen the news?" I asked.

"No... You mean that you've heard about the head?"

"Yes. And it's Max, isn't it? But the Professor and the police scientists have analysed it and they say it's nearly two thousand years old. I don't know how, but it's Max and he's two thousand years old. I hardly dare ask, but was it you who did it?"

My heart was sinking, and a little voice in my head got louder and louder. Don't say it's so, Linn.

"No, Dodd. Though I would be very surprised if the likes of Doctor Ingram were not expecting something of the sort, from what Di told me. I'm not saying that. Whatever happened to Max happened a long time ago. Winter's Gibbett is comparatively new. Close by, you might have seen the stone socket of the old Steng Cross which stood at the highest point of the watershed ridge which the old drove road passed by. Even the cross was not so old - it was from Saxon times - but it marks a place that has been important since before the Romans came. Like I told you when we found the stone in the Mithras temple, maybe the Roman raiding party never made it back home. In a way, some might even think that Max has returned."

"You know what all this means, Linn, don't you? The rock, the cup and ring markings, the pipes, the piper, the music, these burning flames around the hills and valley, all these people."

Linn smiled. "All but the cup and rings. They were before our time. All I know is what my grandfather told me, and that would be what he heard from his grandfather. Hearsay. So I am not sure it's worth anything. I don't think we'll ever know what they really mean. Only what they mean to us."

She paused. "The rest I know. But I don't want to get into trouble again, so I don't think I can tell you any more than I've told you tonight."

"I can wait. For years if you like… Shall we go?"

"I have had a decision to make, Dodd. It's been very difficult. I've been turning it around in my head this last month since I finally got the stone back. It's why I had to go away… You don't see it yourself, Dodd, I don't know why. Maybe it's better that you don't. But you're one of us. That's what brought you back from your travels. That's what draws you to Lordenshaw. It's why you're standing here alongside us now. Come! Place your hand with mine on our cup and ring... I think now's the time."

And the grass grew over the walls and the lights came back on in the valley below Lordenshaw.

THE LEGEND OF LINN RORTING

Local legend has it that in ancient times in north Northumbria, the gods slept below the ground of the Cheviots and surrounding hills. The gateways to their dwelling places were through secret passages in sacred rocks covered with mysterious markings made by the gods themselves thousands of years before. They came and went by day and night without mortal man or woman ever being able to discover their secret entrances. One new moon evening, a beautiful child by the name of Linn Rorting was sitting in the blackness, composing a gentle lament on her pipes on her favourite rock, beyond the safety of the walls of her home on Lordenshaw hill.

Drawn unthinkingly by the unfamiliarity of the melody, the old and distracted god of music appeared from out of the rock, but in so doing, he broke the sacred confidence by revealing his gateway to a mortal. The god so startled the little girl that she lost all memory of her lament. Fearful of the other gods, he made the girl promise never to reveal his doorway to anyone else. In return, he would remind her of the wonderful melody one note at a time on each anniversary new moon, hoping that the melodic sequence would be long enough to outlast her lifetime, and so his error would remain a secret forever.

As the years went by, Linn's memory of her lament was returned to her note by note in an ever-longer duet played out at the secret rock, while at the same time she grew into a beautiful young woman. But then disaster struck. Linn returned at the next anniversary new moon to find the old god curled up dejectedly on what was left of his rock. Someone had cut the stone in half and taken away the part with the secret gateway, leaving the old god of music exiled from his home and also from his sacred pipes which held within them the memory of the lament.

In his anger and despair, the old god held Linn responsible for the crime of other mortals and set her on a quest to locate and replace the stone. At each new moon, she was to return to relate her progress to the old god and if she were ever to succeed, the ending of her melody would be revealed in full on the following new moon. Until then, she would be suspended in a timeless quest.